BLUE BIRD

Paperback ISBN: 978-1-7358110-8-6

Acknowledgments

I'd like to thank:
The Brendans
Alyssa
David
Bits
Kieran

Go to your churches and leave us
philosophers in peace!

—Arthur Schopenhauer

Chapter 1

If, on the contrary, the self does not become itself, it is in despair,
whether it knows it or not.
—Søren Kierkegaard

The bluebirds got to singing at sunrise.

Hello, my friends.

I joined them, squawking my heart out, spilling my rum as young sunlight invaded the dining room. This went on for a while, as it tends to. When my voice finally gave out, I wasn't sure how much time had passed. Time is not a thing a bluebird concerns himself with. We don't live by the clock.

More likely than not, though, I'd woken up Mrs. Connolly again. Hopefully she hadn't called the police. The legal repercussions of another visit from the boys in blue didn't bother me much. It was just another noise complaint. What concerned me more was the possibility of having to see a human being this early in the day. That's never advisable.

Mornings are for the bluebirds.

The underside of my arm stuck to the dining room table as I reached for the bottle. The table is white oak, stained light brown, the same color as a rum and ginger ale. So the drink spillage acts as a kind of glue. It's a rum table. The entire surface is a glistening sheet of goodness.

I used to clean it every now and again, give it a wipe down. But I've come to accept it as a fitting centerpiece to the house. This table is an altar, the eye of the storm. No need to straighten up and momentarily turn into one of those people who keeps a tidy home only to end up back at this table tomorrow, being me, spilling rum and remembering that I quite like Poppy's newspaper clippings bleeding out of every drawer and Nanna's dead house plants withering away in the sun.

It's the way things are.

I became fixated on the three empty chairs at the table. What was the point? Did I expect to have company one day? If I was a pure pragmatist, the table would be far smaller. It would be more of a desk, actually, with a single chair. And instead of a house, I would live in a one-room apartment with a lasagna-friendly microwave.

Why did I need so many rooms?

Upon shallow analysis, one might assume that our tendency toward excess space is simply the result of greed. Those humans love their things. They just want more, more, more. More of everything. But as my eyes jumped between those empty chairs, I had a thought: Extra space means we have more places to hide from ourselves. A chair for this, a chair for that. A room for every activity known to man. We have endless locations to busy ourselves with nonsense, to avoid looking our soul in the eyes.

Throughout history, then, the rich have not lived in castles and estates and palaces only because of greed and ostentation. The kings and khans and emperors and billionaires build mansions because they, more so than any other class of people, are supposed to be happy. They sit atop the societal pyramid. But when the gold doesn't quiet the demons, when the bank account's caress proves insufficient, they add another wing onto the house, a new courtyard, a grand ballroom, a movie theater, a few extra bedrooms. But the novelty of new spaces only lasts so long. Eventually they are greeted by the same old questions that plagued them in the first place, the same questions that plague the rest of us.

Why are you even alive?

Are you happy?

The world told you that the money would make it all better.

Tell me, my lord, has it?

No.

Okay then, not a problem. It must be time to buy an expensive automobile, something with enough horsepower to outrun these questions for good. That means we'll be needing additional garage space too. Call the contractors, dear. We might as well put in a swimming pool while we're at it, and perhaps some more stables for the horses. Yes, that will bring more visitors. Friends help. They always help. Companionship is, at its core, an evading of oneself. The best of friends are merely the best getaway drivers. They know us so well, well enough to keep us far away from ourselves. Honey, how about a guest house too? A place for the relatives to stay for a few weeks per year. They will appreciate that. They are, after all, dodging these very same questions.

I had to get out of the house.

HUGH TWO

I love this bar. I love the torn carpets. I love the shattered mirrors. I love the gaping holes in the ceiling. I love the warped bartop, the drinks gathering in its valleys like lakes. I love the popcorn machine, the way it hisses. I love the aroma of stale beer and overcooked buffalo wings and cigarettes. I love the pool table, that beautiful 1978 Valley. Where are you, seven ball? What paradise have you escaped to? I love Shoe Clue. I love the Beauty and the back alley, the billions of pieces of broken glass. And I love the Sacred Sink. Oh, how I love this sink. I love this whole bar, the entire crumbling operation. Most of all, though, I love the people. I love Gigi and Mr. John and Penny and her annoying little nephew and Edgar and Pancake and Lana and any other person willing to spend time in here and kill themselves slowly. I love all of you. I really do. My only hope is that you can come to feel this on your own, that you can hear these things being shouted by my heart, because you'll never hear it from me....

Chapter 2

The correct standard for judging any man is to remember that
he is really a being who should not exist at all...
—Arthur Schopenhauer

The breeze was blowing in the right direction. The scent of goodness hit me before I even rounded the corner, that unmistakable blend of mildew and popcorn and buffalo wings and cigarettes.

Mr. John was sitting in his metal folding chair just inside the entrance, swaying back and forth to his classical music, staring out the door at the sky. His handheld radio plays at such a low volume that it's a miracle he can hear it over the jukebox.

"Mr. John," I said.

"There is the good boy," he said.

As a seventy-something year old Cambodian man, Mr. John has no business being a bouncer. He's five-foot-two, never checks anyone's ID, and has never once attempted to stop a fight. He just sits there. He's a man of peace.

"Do you have something to smoke for me?" he asked.

I handed him a cigarette.

It took him thirty seconds to light it. It's impossible to discern whether Mr. John moves so slowly because he's old and Asian, and therefore in a state of nirvana, or if he's just geriatric. Perhaps there's little difference.

Gigi had a rum and ginger ale ready for me by the time I sat down in my assigned seat. Pancake immediately plopped down beside me with a tray of popcorn. Half of its contents spilled off onto the warped bartop and got soaked in beer. Without hesitation, he swept the damaged goods onto the floor behind the bar. Gigi threw a lime at him, but he ducked it. I could tell Pancake had something on his mind, that the conversation he was about to have with me had already taken place among himselves.

"You see Joseph A?" he asked, gripping the edge of the bar.

Pancake calls anyone that tries to look put together *Joseph A*, like Joseph A. Bank, the suit store he's certainly never been to. I do believe it's also a nod to Kafka.

Glancing around the bar, I didn't see anyone other than the regulars. Pancake leaned off his stool and scanned down the bar with a squint.

"Where the fuck did this guy go?" he asked himself.

"Bathroom, Sarge," he responded to himself.

"He's probably in the bathroom," he said to me.

"What's his deal?" I asked. "Did he say something to you?"

"Not a fucking word!" shouted Pancake. "But he's watching me, watching everyone. Like a fucking lifeguard. Like we need savin'. He's got it all figured out, this guy, let me tell you." He clearly wanted to rant on, but Gigi brought over a quadruple shot of vodka. More like a half-glass. Some nectar spilled over the rim as Pancake slid it toward himself, creating a suction effect, causing the coaster to cling to the glass. "I don't blame you, pal," he said to the coaster before vacuuming down the liquor. He then paid Gigi in dimes and pennies, re-gripped the bar as if it was his anchor to reality, and got back to it: "There's not a snowball's chance in hell this guy's in here because he just oh-so loves the scenery. Yeah, I'm sure he just can't wait to chat it up with Penny about the ins and outs of diabetes. We're chimps to this guy! He's at the zoo, watching us, as if he's got all the fucking answers!" It took all the power in his necrotic lungs to get his statement out. He started coughing onto my hand as I went digging into the popcorn, so I shifted my excavation efforts to the other side of the tray.

"You got gaspers?" he asked.

I lit him up a cigarette.

He smoked a quarter of the cigarette with his first drag and was still sucking down smoke when I suggested that this Joseph A might be with the health board, here to do the annual inspection. He nodded twice at the idea and removed the cigarette from his mouth for just long enough to say, "Could be," then kept inhaling. By the time he finished his first pull, half the cigarette was gone. He rubbed the fallen ashes into his pants and exhaled so much smoke that I could barely see him. From behind the plume, he said, "Fucking lifeguard either way."

The bathroom door swung open and out came Joseph A. Pancake was right, someone like this didn't walk into Hugh Two unless they were lost, serving a warrant, or here to slap the perpetual C health rating on the murky front window. This guy was a top-of-the-line Joseph A. He was an older man, probably late 40s or early 50s, wearing a button-down shirt, nice pants, and shiny shoes. And he had a cockiness about him, a contented smile. What really bothered me most was the contentedness. The man was comfortable. He really thought he belonged here.

Pancake visually assaulted him as he passed us, but Joseph A didn't give us the time of day. It wasn't until he took a seat in the stool closest to the front door, presumably to have the best vantage point, that he glanced our way and gave us a quick nod of the head.

"Lifeguard motherfucker," said Pancake.

"Thinks he's hot shit," he responded to himself.

"Not after we get through with him," he tacked on.

"You gunna fuck him up?" I asked.

"Oh, we're gunna give him his," said Pancake, cramming a fistful of popcorn into his mouth.

"We as in you and me?" I asked.

"No, me and Lana. I'm gunna go wake her up out at the Beauty," he said with fiery sarcasm. "Yes, me and you, you fuck! Who do you think I mean?"

"I thought you meant...you," I said.

"Oh, like I'm some loony fuck?" he yelled in my face. "Are you gunna go lifeguard on me too? You here to save me from me, myself, and I?!"

"Pancake, I'm with you here," I assured him.

"I know that. I know, okay? I just—" As he clutched the bar, gathering his thoughts, a fly landed on his forehead. He froze, remaining perfectly still. The fly did the same. This lasted a minute or two.

"I think he wants to stay," I said.

"We all do," said Pancake. He blew a gentle upward breeze from his mouth, sending the fly buzzing away, then glared at Joseph A: "This fucking guy with that shirt and his shoes and the whole way he's doing things." He leaned back in his chair and whistled at Joseph A. "Suck a dick, Joey-boy!"

"Pancake, take it easy," said Gigi.

Pancake ignored her, continuing to berate Joseph A. At one point, Mr. John actually got up from his chair beside the entrance. I thought it might be his first attempt at preemptive action—or action of any kind—but he simply applied billiards hand chalk to his underarms to eliminate moisture, then sat back down and repeatedly nodded to himself as he felt the powder doing its job, drying up the sweat.

"You got any beans?" I asked, hoping to distract Pancake from violence.

"I'm beanless Joe Jackson," he said.

"Okay, well let's get some more popcorn," I said. "I'll get Edgar to melt us some butter, some buffalo sauce—"

"The Mixture."

"The good shit, yea," I said. "And we'll shoot some pool. No need to jump into anything with this guy right now." But the better half of me knew that if we stuck around late enough into the night, we wouldn't be able to help ourselves. The drinks would win.

Pancake muttered to himself, weighing my proposal.

"I'll buy your drinks," I offered.

He muttered some more, his grunts sounding closer and closer to approval.

"Double vodka," I said to Gigi.

"Triple," said Pancake.

"If the guy's still here at closing, we'll fuck him up," I said.

"Rain," said Pancake.

* * *

The popcorn machine has a consistent digestive cycle. You feed it kernels, it cooks them, the popcorn is eaten, then, once empty, the machine begs for more. It hisses and whines for about ten minutes, then starts to cook itself, burning away at the buttery residue and rejected kernels. I'm pretty sure a normal machine would have a sensor and automatically stop cooking, but that would be a real shame. The scent of popcorn-machine autophagy is a Hugh Two staple. And it was mighty strong tonight.

It was 1:30am.

By my count, we'd played 26 games of pool, with me winning 23 of them. On most occasions, Pancake and I are very evenly matched. From a talent perspective, he's light-years ahead of me. He taught me everything I know about pool, and at times he's downright masterful. When I first met him, he told me he was living above a pool hall in San Pedro. It wasn't until I went there with him that I realized he meant this literally: He lived on the roof. Anyway, sessions like these, when I'm able to dominate him, happen for two possible reasons, both of which applied tonight.

Reason one, Pancake's minds become obsessed with something else. Currently, the flavor of the night was our looming confrontation with Joseph A. For a guy with multiple personalities, Pancake cannot multitask. It's one of his finest qualities: pure integrity. He can't speak passionately about something without marrying his words to action. He can't fake it. He is his own sovereign state. He makes the laws, swings the gavel, and doles out the floggings. But if he decrees something, any temporal gap between the proclamation itself and the carrying out of necessary sentencing burns his soul. So the 26 games of pool were only a traffic jam en route to the main showdown against Joseph A.

Reason two was a simpler one: Before we started playing, Pancake went out to the Beauty to smoke meth. He usually doesn't announce it when he heads out for a blast, but you can smell the meth fumes on him. One might think the amphetamines would help his focus, but they don't. It transforms his game into a rapid-fire form of pinball. He spends no time lining up shots and slams the ball 100mph. Zero strategy. The more destruction he can cause, the better. And he parlays every shot into an air guitar solo with the pool cue.

"Kaboomba!" he shouted, smashing the cue ball.

I stepped up and sank the eight ball to win the game, but Pancake wasn't even looking. He was busy strumming out the final cords of "Kashmir" by Led Zeppelin, dropping to his knees as the song came to a close, screaming at Joseph A: "I'm drowning, Mr. Lifeguard!"

In stormed Lana from the back door. "Where the fuck is it?!" she screamed at Pancake.

"Did you check your pockets?" he replied.

Lana slapped him across the face. It was solid, jarring contact.

"Holy marlin," said Pancake. "That one happened."

Lana scurried over to me, grabbing me by the collar. "Where is it?"

"Why don't you just sit down and grab a drink?" I said.

"Fuck you," she said, threatening to slap me. "Both of you can suck a fuck. A dick, a dick. Suck a dick, that's what I meant."

Lana stomped around the bar and foraged for her missing left shoe. Always the left one. She checked all the usual stash spots: under the bathroom sink, behind the popcorn machine, hanging from a side-view mirror out front, on top of the claw machine. One time we actually hung it like an ornament from the fake Christmas tree and it was there for three days until Penny ratted us out. No one seems to know exactly how long the tree has been set up, but legend says more than a decade straight. All the ornaments have been stolen, replaced with Budweiser bottles, cigarette boxes, a few bras, some empty cans of beans.

"You sure you had one on that foot tonight?" asked Pancake at one point with what seemed to be full sincerity.

Did he not remember us going out to the Beauty earlier and stealing her shoe while she was nodding out? I couldn't tell if he was kidding. He even seemed concerned, like he might join Lana in the search.

Lana ended up smacking Pancake a few more times and storming out the back door, making this one of the finest games of Shoe Clue I had ever witnessed. We'd gone entirely against our usual pattern and hidden her shoe in plain sight, right on the bar where she normally sits. When she eventually came back in and had a drink, the shoe was there, and she had a good laugh with us. That's how it goes, usually. None of the regulars can get too angry at each other. Everyone fucks up someone's day at some point, so there's no use playing the saint. The shoe always turns up.

"You two want anything before I close up?" asked Gigi.

"We want the world, Gigi-baby!" shouted Pancake.

"Two double vodkas," he followed up in a British whisper.

I nodded at her: Rum.

"You two have to promise not to cause trouble," she said.

"Ten-four," said Pancake.

"We'll be good," I told her.

Joseph A stood up and headed toward the bathroom. At this point, I was shocked that he was still around. Pancake had been taunting him all night. But Joey-boy had kept his distance and remained silent. As he passed us, we both eyed him like wolves, strung out on slow-cooked hatred and liquor. This guy had probably found Hugh Two on the internet and decided to stop in to reassure himself that, in his bullshit universe, there are good people and bad people, and he's one of the good ones.

At one point earlier in the night he even walked over to the popcorn machine just to stare at it. It was as though he needed a close enough look to solidify to himself that he would never in his life eat out of anything so filthy.

That was the turning point for me, his popcorn machine assessment. I switched from hoping he would leave to praying he'd be around come closing time.

"Penny, play what we like, darling!" shouted Pancake.

Penny's stool next to the jukebox is a blessing and a curse. Music duty. She took a brief hiatus from scratching away at a scratch-off ticket, the closest she gets to cardiovascular exercise, and spun her stool to the right to navigate the jukebox and play something by Frankie.

"Trapped in the bathroom," said Pancake. "Joey-boy's a rat in a cage."

We tapped our glasses.

I chugged my rum.

"Smoke," says Pancake.

As I light him up a cigarette, the opening of "It's All Over" by Frankie Miller comes on, with the volume cranked to the max. Wonderful choice, Penny. I glance her way to give her a nod of approval, but she's already back to scratching away at her scratch-offs, the blaring music vibrating the fat on the backs of her arms.

White dust starts falling.

When the jukebox is loud enough, it shakes this bar by the bones, knocking loose a gentle mist of plaster and asbestos from the ceiling.

Pancake heads toward the bathroom, and I trail him. He grabs a pool stick and snaps it over his knee in stride, holding the wooden shank with one hand and yanking the bathroom door open with the other.

In we go.

It's empty.

I quietly try to open the stall.

It's locked.

Even better: We're going to storm Joseph A while his pants are down, exposing himself for a pool stick clubbing. Pancake gestures for me to pause. He props open the bathroom door with the garbage can so that we can properly hear Frankie. He shoots me a wild glance. Time for blood. He is a wolf, a starving animal. His eyes are those of a man in touch with his deepest instincts, a son of the caves. There is violence in all of us, and it's a shame to always keep the monster at bay.

Pancake charges the stall door, smashing his shoulder through it. It breaks clean off the hinges. He lifts the pool stick over his head but freezes.

He's heartbroken, devastated.

I scurry up behind him to get a view.

It's Lana, hunched over on the toilet. The women's room must have been occupied. She certainly just shot some heroin. She's nodding out, appearing to repeatedly die, fading into the ultimate warmth. Her eyes flutter.

Most of us will never be that happy.

"My Silver," she whispers upon seeing Pancake.

"Goddamnit, Lana!" shouts Pancake. He bashes the pool stick against the wall. For a second, I think he might beat her to death, or me, just because his mind had so committed to impending violence that anything short of bloodshed won't do. He stands perfectly still. His breathing slows, a stillness comes over him, his eyes domesticate themselves.

"Are you okay?" he asks Lana.

She throws a real nod among the rhythm of her heroin nods.

"Good," says Pancake. He runs his hand through her hair, then leans down and slips off her left shoe, handing it to me. "Find a place for this." He drops his billiard shank and lifts Lana into his arms. "Let's get you out to the Beauty," he says. Lana's feet drag on the floor, leaving train tracks in the filth as he carries her out.

Ah, the Sacred Sink.

Drip, drip, drip.

Constant and steady.

Drip, drip, drip.

A metronome to degeneracy.

Almighty God...have you read Nietzsche?

I am where I should be.

Lana's heroin baggie floats in the toilet.

Flies buzz overhead.

Lavatory vultures, that's what they are.

I wish I could stay forever, right here in The Ruthless Now.

CITIES

Too many people come to cities for the wrong reason. They can't find happiness in their little hometown, so they pack up their bags and head for the big city hoping to find all of the things they love in one place. But this is a selfish mindset, one that misses the point. The greatest value of a city isn't the cuisine or the transportation system or the sports franchises. The real beauty of city life is the opportunity to be humbled, to be appalled. Within a few blocks, one should see countless things one disagrees with. A good city assaults you, not always metaphorically. This is the gold, the brutal honesty that comes from living among millions. A good city should let you know that you're insignificant. You are one shard of glass in an endless mosaic. Your opinions are small and disposable and probably unoriginal. Yes, if you work hard, you could become the president of a bank and buy a penthouse. On the way to your office, though, a homeless man can push you in front of a train because he didn't like the way your tie was talking to him. It will be a tragedy, but a brief one. Within the week, you will not be missed. Someone else will have your job. Your apartment will be sold. In the big picture, you were nothing more than a train delay. You are a very, very small part of this operation. Things will go on just fine without you....

Chapter 3

My final memory from last night was planning to fight Joseph A.

But I woke up in the middle of the day with no signs of defeat, no cuts or scrapes or black eyes, so I assumed the brawl didn't happen. They say anything can happen in a fight, but I haven't found that to be the case. I have never won. My tendency to fight stronger, more sober opponents seems to eliminate all chances of an upset. It's a rigged system. The house always wins. But at this point, I don't mind it. Losing fights is a tradition. I'd feel ashamed to turn my back on it.

I made a deal with my hangover at the dining room table. We negotiated over rum and eventually arrived at the same arrangement we always reach: He agreed to come back tomorrow, I agreed to absolutely nothing.

This is my house.

See yourself out.

The peace that comes after a few drinks is the greatest feeling life has to offer. A shot of heroin or arriving at the peak of Mount Everest might be more blissful, a momentary Eden, but that's the problem. They're too good, too rapturous and ephemeral. They're like a tropical vacation. The sun is shining, stress does not exist. But in the back of your mind, hiding behind the joy, is reality: This can only last so long. I will have to check out soon enough. Back to the routine. Back to the misery. But a couple of drinks brings about a cozy goodness, a place that itself is a kind of home, somewhere you could stay forever.

I heard Pancake's cart rolling down the block. Out the front window, I saw him roll up with a bop in his step and parallel park his shopping cart. He *beep, beep, beeped* as he slowly backed in, intentionally bumping the shiny vehicle in front of him, and then stepped away to observe his work. I don't know what he was saying, but he was rambling, gesticulating at the cart, likely congratulating himself about his park job.

I opened the door as he walked up the porch stairs.

"I need your help with something," he said.

"Something big, Sarge," he added in a raspy voice.

"I'm not really looking to go big just yet," I said.

"There are things," he said.

"What things?"

"Certain things," he said.

"What kind of things?"

"You got any weed?" he asked.

"No," I said. "It's been giving me panic attacks."

"Jesus, Mary, and Josephina!" he cried in frustration. "I've been trying to get high for the last thirty miles!" He slammed his hand on the wooden banister. It cracked.

"I've got rum," I said.

"Of course you do, Blackbeard," he said.

He strolled past me into the house. Spotting my cell phone on the dining room table, he threw it on the ground. "Not on my watch," he said. I shouldn't have left it out given Pancake's abhorrence for all things internet. He disappeared into the kitchen. I heard him open the microwave.

"Holy marlin," he whispered, then he screamed, "Nagasaki!"

I shuffled into the kitchen. The microwave was destroyed, black residue caked on every wall. Pancake peeled off a piece of the charred matter and tasted it. After a moment of calibration, he said, "Cheese."

"Lasagna," I said.

"This place could've been Rome in 64," he said with a grin, as if it was a shame that I hadn't burned the house to the ground. He plucked some more debris from the microwave and chewed it, crunching it between his teeth.

"That sounds like the container," I said.

"Number five," he nodded. "Polypropylene."

* * *

Pancake locked his cart to a telephone pole. He then removed his shoes, hung them over the side of the cart, and bellowed, "Hands off, Jeremiah!"

I didn't see a Jeremiah in the area.

The bells on the door jingled as we entered Port Liquor.

Amir immediately said, "No." He shuffled out from behind the counter to stop us.

"He's got rupees, Amir," said Pancake, gesturing to me. "We're gunna get a few things, so save the fucking gospel."

I went into the bathroom and took a piss.

When I came out, Amir was screaming. "Get them out, I say! Get them out right now!"

Pancake was barefoot, boxing out Amir basketball-style, preventing him from getting to the microwave. "Protect the low key!" he shouted.

"Again he puts his clothes in the microwave!" yelled Amir to me. "He is not permitted, no, no, no!"

I watched and laughed, but it hurt my head. So I let them duke it out and grabbed myself a few shooters and a can of ginger ale.

Beep! went the microwave. Pancake gave Amir one final shove to create some separation, then snatched his socks from the microwave and bolted out the door. I was waiting at the counter when Amir returned in defeat.

"Why do you hang out with that one?" he asked me.

"He's a good guy," I said.

"How is he good?"

"I need some time to think about that," I said.

"He's no good," said Amir.

"He's not that bad."

"Last week, he cooked his underpants," said Amir.

"That's bad," I conceded, "on a scale of things."

"He steals," said Amir.

"He's a good rebounder too," I said.

Amir had no idea what I was talking about. He pointed to the door: "Do not return."

Pancake was sitting on the concrete outside, putting his shoes back on.

"What, your socks were wet?" I asked.

"Not particularly." He tied a nautical grade knot in his shoelaces. "It'll dry 'em out if you need it, if you're in a pinch. But it's really about nuking the bacteria. Microorganisms."

"Are they nice and warm?" I asked.

"Oh baby," he said, hopping to his feet. "Off to the Ravine."

"For what?"

"I need your help, fuckmill," he said.

"Yes, yes," he reminded himself. "The plan." He unlocked his cart.

"I thought the plan was that you needed a microwave," I said.

"That was preliminary," he said. "Other things are happening."

"What things?"

"Infringement," he said.

"Is this about Joseph A?" I asked.

"No, no," he said. "Joey-boy's a whole other issue. We'll get around to dear Joey." He rolled away his cart and muttered something to a fire hydrant. None of it made sense.

I followed him.

* * *

If you've never seen the L.A. River, picture a wide concrete drainage ditch. Its hideous water runs through the center of Los Angeles and dumps into the Pacific. The farther south you get, the dirtier the water becomes. By the time it reaches us down here in Long Beach, it's a majestic green-brown, with nuclear patches of algae growing along its concrete bottom.

It's a gorgeous river, the intestinal tract of a festering city, a passing of the pollution buck to the fishes while knowing full well it'll come back to bite us in the end. The Romans had their aqueducts to pump fresh water into cities. We have the L.A. River to funnel out all the soda bottles and feces and tinfoil and brake dust and lawn chairs and those thin waxy paper bags that street churros are served in.

Right in the heart of this filth, just a few miles north of the Port of Long Beach, you'll find what the homeless call the Ravine, an overgrown stretch near Willow Street. The fact that plants and fish and humans can survive here is proof that God better bring the heavy artillery if he wants to wage a successful doomsday. Life survives.

Pancake fluffed up the pillows in his riverside tent, then gestured for me to enter. "Go to sleep," he said.

"How long is this gunna take?" I asked.

"Just close the eyes for a bit." As he tried to exit the tent and make way for me, he knocked over his can of beans with his foot, spilling them across the tent floor.

"For God's sake, Pancake," said Lana.

"I've got it handled," said Pancake. He quickly swept the loose beans back into the can. Lana sidestepped around him, ducking into the tent like a ballerina. She mopped up the bean juice with a towel, disposed of it beneath the mattress, then gracefully glided back out of the tent.

"Your highness," she said, ushering me into the tent.

I crouched inside. I'd been to the Ravine plenty of times, but I'd never actually come inside their tent. It was shockingly tidy: a thick foam pad with navy bedding, a wooden crate of books, a hanging lantern, a utility bin with flashlights, bug spray, and paper towels. I laid down, and Lana tucked me in.

"The idea is for it to feel organic," she said.

"Bags under the eyes," said Pancake.

"And water under the bridge!" he sang, holding the note for so long that Lana had to put her hand over his mouth.

"If he shows up and you're just hanging out in here," said Lana, "it won't seem legitimate. But if you're genuinely asleep, he'll buy it. He'll assume we abandoned the tent and moved somewhere else, and you took over."

I nodded. I always find it baffling to interact with Lana early in the day. She's a perfectly rational and intelligent human being. It made me want to ask her how she ended up here. But if I waited until her first heroin hit, the question would answer itself.

"What time is he supposed to come?" I asked.

"Today," said Pancake between bean chugs, juice dripping through his beard.

"Just act like you own the place," said Lana.

"Beans?" offered Pancake.

I shook my head.

Lana zipped up the tent.

"Where are you guys gunna go?" I asked.

"North," said Pancake.

* * *

Whoop! Whoop!

I woke up and peered out of a small gash in the tent.

Up on the embankment above the river, slowing driving along the bike path, was a police car. It came to a stop. I heard the window roll down, followed by someone whistling to me.

I stayed in the tent.

Whoop! Whoop!

I finished off my flask and slipped it among Pancake's books.

I saw Kafka.

"Don't make me come down there!" shouted the officer.

I unzipped the tent and stepped out.

"Where are the others?" he asked.

"What others?"

"You know who I'm talking about."

"Sir, I just woke up. You'll have to excuse me."

He began descending the concrete embankment of the river, one hand on his belt. I knew instantly who this man was. A version of him exists in every workplace across the world. This is an individual who takes his occupation so seriously that even the boss of the company, the police commissioner in his case, ought to pull him aside and tell him to calm the fuck down. It's just a job. Get a life.

"Where are your friends?" he asked.

"I'd love to know what you're talking about, Officer…" I leaned in to read his badge, "Nellins. Because to be honest, I could use some companionship, but—"

"Save the bullshit, imbecile," said Nellins.

"Imbecile, wow."

"That's what you are."

"Yeah, no, I understand. It's just been a while since I've heard the term."

He bumped shoulders with me on his way to the tent, then began rummaging through it. It was a pathetic attempt at protocol. He desperately wanted it to be methodical and procedural, but he kept fumbling and tripping over himself. He bumped his head on the hanging lamp and tossed it out onto the ground outside the tent.

"Chandelier," I said.

He should have just accepted the whole situation for what it was: a joke. He was ransacking the tent of an impostor homeless man beside a fake river in a city with an astronomically high crime rate. Murders were happening, humans were being trafficked, kilos of heroin were flowing in through the port. Go do something useful.

When a situation so clearly wants to be called comedy but you insist on treating it as tragedy, you become the joke. But Officer Nellins refused to laugh. He rifled through everything, making a mess of the tent, forcing himself to keep moving because if he stopped to observe himself and think he would remember that he was a low-ranking police officer searching a six-by-six camping tent and not a top-secret operative on the verge of solving the JFK assassination once and for all.

Out he came with the smoking gun: my flask. He uncapped it and turned it over.

Not one drop came out.

"Whoever it was," I commented. "He must have been thorough."

This comment solidified the hatred. Nellins glared right through me. This was a man who had watched too many movies. His parents never sat him down and told him the good stuff: He did not matter, nor did his wife or his badge or his values, his education or his children. We were acting in two separate plays, he and I. In his story, he was the hero. In mine, there were none.

"What the hell are you doing here?" he asked.

"Sleeping."

He stepped closer and placed his hand on his baton. "Where do you live?"

"Here."

"No, you don't," he said.

"Why would I be in a tent if I had a place to live?"

"ID," he said.

"I don't have one."

He aggressively patted me down. "What's your name?"

I gave him my name.

He disappeared into his police cruiser to look me up. He likely saw a few macro-level details: a drunken misdemeanor from years ago, a slew of traffic violations, a recent house call because I was a bluebird.

A few minutes later he exited his cruiser and walked to the edge of the bike path, looking down on me, posturing himself heroically. Some people know their ideas aren't memorable, so they must get the body involved, make things physical: puff the chest, wave the arms, point a finger.

"If you're still here when I come back," he announced, "I will arrest you."

I did a military salute.

"I know who you are," he said.

"Very good," I said.

It was time to clean up the tent.

BARTENDERS

The best bartenders care just enough. They care enough to talk to you but not enough to be your therapist while other patrons go thirsty. Serve drinks: This is the number one commandment of bartending. It's the golden rule, no exceptions. A man without a drink is a dangerous thing. If one patron is dying of a heart attack and twelve are dying of thirst, you serve the twelve. You're not a paramedic. You're a fucking bartender. Any moron can save a life. It takes brilliance to destroy a dozen. So, we salute you, my dearest Gigi....

Chapter 4

Highly organized research is guaranteed to produce nothing new.
—Frank Herbert

I poured a touch of ginger ale into my flask. Some rum was in there, waiting.

"Can you spare a dollar?" asked a young homeless man.

"I don't have one."

"What about some change?"

"I paid with a credit card."

"What about cigarettes? Do you smoke?"

"I might," I responded. "But why should I give you one?"

He grew skittish and switched on the puppy dog eyes.

This was probably an act, but I still felt bad, because I didn't know this man. A stranger can steal empathy from you. You have to know someone to properly neglect him. So I introduced myself and gave him a cigarette as the first step toward never giving him one again.

Now was his chance to reciprocate, to prove he understood the dynamics of human exchange. These interactions are an audition. If I had failed to give him a smoke, I would have failed by his standards. But I had passed. I provided value. I fulfilled my part of the contract. Now it was his turn to promote my happiness. There are infinite ways to do it.

"I really appreciate it," he said.

That wasn't one of the options.

I left.

Your fake gratitude does nothing for me. Most people think too narrowly about economics. It's not all dollars and cents, booze and cigarettes. The market has a soul. Human interaction has no concrete exchange rates, no producer and consumer. Life is the currency, and it can be created from thin air. Make me laugh. Dispense some street wisdom. Throw me a good one-liner. Disgust me. Tell me a story. Better yet, let's become a story, you and I. I'll give you the whole pack of cigarettes if you shank me in the abdomen with a broken-off umbrella handle. That's a fair trade, so long as I live to tell the tale.

Just because you live in the gutter doesn't mean you can't bring value. In fact, if you become so convinced that the only way to bring value is through labor or cash or property, you're delusional, homeless or not. It's quite amazing, though, that the American system can make a pure capitalist out of someone with zero capital and no prospect of acquiring it other than pestering me outside of the liquor store. I did understand, of course, that the man was just trying to survive. He probably had a tough childhood. He seemed profoundly sad. But if every profoundly sad person loitered outside the store and pleaded for cigarettes, society wouldn't exist. The beggars would outnumber the buyers. Looting would ensue.

But that's the problem with these flocks of hobos over here in the Downtown area: They want your money, your compassion, and a job offer that'll lift them out of the gutter for six months until they relapse and end up right back on the same corner with a nicer tent, stronger heroin, and a sadder sob story that's bound to pull in more cash and tears than the last one. They seem unaware of the carousel on which they ride.

I prefer the homeless that live on the outskirts of the city. They don't set up shop near busy intersections or crowded train stations and play the sympathy card for a living. They find a remote location and build a life. They're self-sufficient. They're go-getters. That's why I love Pancake. He never begs. If he needs something, he steals it. He takes care of himselves.

* * *

Gigi is like a musician.

She feels out the room, getting a pulse on everyone's mood and blood alcohol content. If she senses that you need a drink quickly, that every second without the medicine is a struggle, she moves like lightning, with minimal loss of skill. But if your buzz is appropriate and you're feeling up to the grave challenge of waiting sixty seconds for the antidote, she'll make a ceremony of it.

So that's what she was doing.

"Well?" she asked.

"Just thinking," I said.

"About?"

"Not much."

"Liar," she said, threatening me with the soda hose.

"I'm thinking about how you make drinks," I said. "Your awareness."

"Here it comes," she said.

"It dawned on me that you're kind of like a hibachi chef. You've gotta have a feel for how hungry the crowd is, you know? If you start seeing a customer eyeing the food, getting a little gluttonous on you, you've gotta step your pace up, cook a little faster, maybe pop the guy a round of grilled veggies. You know how they do that, the hibachi chefs? The veggie pop. How they toss you pieces of broccoli and onions off the spatula?"

"You're retarded," said Gigi.

"I don't like when you use that word," said Penny from down the bar.

"I know," said Gigi. "It just slips out sometimes. I'm not proud of it."

"You never know who might be hurt by it," said Penny. "A lot of people have family members or friends with, you know, mental issues. Some people are born slow. They can't help it."

"I'd never say it around someone who's actually retarded," said Gigi.

"So I'm not in fact retarded," I said.

"No, you are," retorted Gigi.

"Yeah," agreed Penny. "For you, it makes sense."

I gestured to a stray piece of popcorn on the bar and opened my mouth. Gigi played hibachi chef, grabbing the popcorn and tossing it my way. It was a good shot, pinpoint accurate, with a generous arc. I had plenty to work with, but I botched it.

"You don't deserve a drink," she said as she gave me my drink.

Gigi is in her late forties and slightly overweight. But she's a wholesome woman, a pure soul. She's very special to me. First of all, she makes the drinks. But there's something beyond that, something more profound and matriarchal. It has something to do with how she treats everyone like they're nothing. I may be worthless to her, yes, but so are the rest. What she makes me feel is not hate or love, but reality. There's no chance I'll ever be anything more than a guy she pours drinks for, and I cherish her for that.

I played a few games of pool against myself. In any craft, practicing alone is supposedly the key to being a champion. We must put in the hard work when no one is watching. But I must be cut from non-champion cloth, because I can't muster any enthusiasm unless I'm competing against someone else. I find no enjoyment in defeating myself, in telling myself I am better than I was yesterday. I was good yesterday, and I'm good today. I just need someone else to pick up a pool stick and accept the role of loser. No one else was keen on playing though, so I settled for mindlessly hitting balls around the table. It gave me something to do other than worry and smoke cigarettes.

"Like totally free?" I heard a fat man say from over by the popcorn machine.

"Look at the sign," said his hefty girlfriend. "It says it's free."

Delighted, the two of them began harvesting tray after tray of popcorn, stuffing their faces. They lingered by the machine and gazed into it as if they'd found the holy grail. How generous it was of the bar to offer free snacks, they raved. I strongly considered telling them that the popcorn machine has nothing to do with generosity. It's about providing the patrons just enough sustenance to keep them conscious and drinking. This is a watering hole, folks, not a snack bar. Please save some rations for the rest of us.

Penny waddled over to the popcorn machine to refill her tray. She sized up the blubbery couple and, as if saying hello, said, "Diabetes?" They weren't sure if it was a statement or a question, so Penny continued: "I have Type 1 myself." Then, with no shortage of pride, she said, "I'd have worked my way into Type 2 either way."

I heard Pancake *beep, beep, beeping* out back in the alley. Then he started shouting: "Heave-ho! Heave-ho!" His voice echoed into the bar.

"¡Ándale, Ádale!" he added, jumping to a higher pitch.

It sounded like a cockfight was going on back there. Glancing out the back door, I realized it was nighttime. This was news to me.

I strolled out into the alley.

Trash was everywhere: broken bottles, cans, newspapers, cardboard, dog shit, chicken wing remnants, orange peels, human shit, broken furniture. Pancake was sweeping out the Beauty's rusted interior with Mr. John's broom. The Beauty is an abandoned 1980s Honda Civic with no seats that serves as a place to pass out, shoot up, smoke meth, or contemplate the long string of mistakes that are commonly referred to as your life. How the Beauty got here, no one knows. It could very well predate the bar itself.

"A little spring cleaning?" I asked.

"Is it spring?" asked Pancake.

"Not sure," I said.

"She looks good," he said.

"Real good, Sarge," he agreed.

"You need help?" I asked.

"Do your chores," he said, pointing the broom at the multicolored quilt hanging on the dumpster. I grabbed it. The edges of the blanket have been cut to account for the wheel wells, so it perfectly matches the car's floor plan. We spread the quilt out across the cab, making sure the side with yellow squares on it was facing up. I don't know why this is the way it goes, but it is. There's a protocol. It's best not to question it.

"Can't ask for more," said Pancake, admiring the Beauty.

"You really can't," I said.

"If you do," said Pancake. "You should be hanged."

"Off to the gallows!" I shouted in an English accent.

Pancake looked me up and down, nodding with endorsement. Sensing it coming, I closed my eyes and accepted a healthy smack across the face.

The back door to the kitchen cracked. Edgar propped it open with his wooden two-by-four, painted blue, that says *recuerda* on it in silver paint. Another timeless system. Smoke began billowing out the door. I could hear him watching a soccer game on his tiny television, the commentators shouting in Spanish.

Pancake approached the door and said, "Fuego, Papi."

Edgar's hand popped out the door with a cigarette. Pancake grabbed it. Next came a lighter. Edgar sparked it. Pancake leaned in, lit his smoke, and said, "Gracias por nada."

"How are we doing on the Mixture?" I asked Edgar.

"There is plenty, brother," he said.

His hand soon came out with a plastic side cup of the glorious concoction. Before I could tell him that I was just checking on supply, that we didn't have any popcorn to pour it over, Pancake snatched the cup and drank it down, leaving him with a melted butter-buffalo sauce mustache.

"That fuck's not in there, is he?" asked Pancake.

Edgar swung the door fully open and joined us in the alley. "Which fuck do you talk about?"

"Joseph A," said Pancake.

"You're still on this?" I asked.

"Like height on a kite!" barked Pancake.

Of course he was still on it. Pancake's laws are divinely inspired by the highest power in the realm: himself. Ideals were at stake. Time meant nothing. Wars had only beginnings. One time a woman called Pancake a filthy pig outside Port Liquor. He waited weeks for her to return, then trailed her home. He smashed her windshield with a garden gnome and left a strip of bacon under her windshield wiper like a parking ticket. When I sarcastically suggested that it was a weak response, he retorted that he didn't want to blow the whole pack of bacon in one go.

"Which Joseph A do you mean?" asked Edgar.

"The fuck that was here the other night," said Pancake.

"Tall guy with a collared shirt," I clarified.

"Oh, collars on the shirt, yes," said Edgar. "I know the one."

"Guy thinks he's something," said Pancake.

"He thinks he's Papi," I said. "But there's only room for one Papi around here."

Edgar touched my chest with gratitude. "The man with the collars," he said. "I know where he likes to hang out."

* * *

Edgar got off at midnight and we followed him up Daisy, the apartment buildings getting more decrepit by the block. By my estimation, domestic disputes raged in about a quarter of the homes. Women yelled, men yelled, children cried. The current subject of these fights wasn't money, but most of them had undoubtedly started with money.

The key ingredient for any clash is a spark, and the poor always have one: finances. It starts with the bank. Then lovers are free to swing the battlefront to any other topic. They can rekindle old arguments. They can concoct new ones on the fly. You cheated on me eleven years ago. Okay, well, you're starting to look overweight. And I hate your sister. In fact, I hate most of your family. The goal here is to end up at your partner's jugular. Nothing is off the table. Why hold back? You're broke and hungry and fighting for your life. Show no mercy. Mercy is for the rich.

"What did he do?" asked Edgar. "Mr. Joseph A."

"Many things," said Pancake. "Violation upon violation, stacked to the moon."

"What's this place called that we're going to?" I asked.

"It has the name Christina's," said Edgar. "On Anaheim."

"I know the place," said Pancake.

"They got a spigot out back, no?" he asked himself.

Edgar went to respond, not realizing this chat was between Pancake and Pancake.

"Yes, yes, they do," barked Pancake. "Good pressure, Sarge." He scurried ahead and disappeared.

We passed a liquor store, so I went in and came out with a few shooters for myself and a tallboy of Modelo for Edgar. He cracked open his beer and took a long, emotional sip. He's the type to think drinks should be earned. Work a long shift, get rewarded with a cold beer. It's a healthy outlook, with an innocence to it.

"I love this place," said Edgar.

"Which one?"

"This city," he said. "Long Beach."

"Oh yeah, me too," I said. "It's the greatest city on the planet. It's nice and terrible."

"Yes, a good place and bad place," he said. "There is the ocean and there is the other things." He gently grazed his hand on a dilapidated couch left to rot on the sidewalk. "It is the place for me."

"The place for us, Papi," I said.

"Yes," he said. "The place for us."

"Live fast, die middle-aged," I said, holding up my shooter for a cheers.

Edgar nodded and tapped his drink on mine, sidestepping some dog shit.

We drank to the rhythm of marital woes and aging mufflers, barking chihuahuas and hungry babies. We were just two damaged men who felt warm in the arms of a broken city. Everything was fucked, and we were the nuts and bolts.

"May I ask you something?" he asked.

Christ. I immediately recognized my mistake: I had gotten too sentimental. I had let the dreamy silence swallow us. This had become a moment between us. We'd bonded. I saw it in Edgar's eyes. He was ready to dig deeper with a piercing question, like why I hang out with the homeless or why I drink to the point of amnesia or why I have seemingly no purpose in life.

"What is a spigot?" he asked.

* * *

Christina's was the Hispanic equivalent of Hugh Two.

There were three seating options: the bar, the floor, or plastic lawn chairs around fold-up tables. It looked like an impromptu tailgate. There were big water jugs, like you'd see on the sidelines of an athletic event, all over the place. The dozen or so patrons, some of whom looked like actual 1800s Mexican caballeros, eyed me in astonishment. It wasn't animosity. It was authentic confusion as to why I would come to such a place. It was as though they considered me above it. This offended me greatly.

Off in the corner, behind an old pool table, were the mandatory statues of Jesus and the Virgin Mary, with a few religious paintings on the walls above them. These set ups are a staple in the Hispanic establishments of Los Angeles. It doesn't matter whether you're walking into a laundromat, a mechanic, or a dentist, respects will be paid to the Lord. No matter how crammed the space, a shrine must fit. I've seen them under tables, in back alleys, on top of refrigerators. Often there are even satellite worship chambers in the bathrooms. Hispanics decorate as if tomorrow is the Second Coming. When Christ returns to Earth, they'll be ready to point to their shrine and insist they're with the good guys.

Thankfully Edgar knew everyone in the bar. He did the rounds while I sampled some of the huge water jugs. They were filled with a sweet yellowish elixir that was stronger than fuck.

"Three dollars," said the bartender.

"What is this?" I asked her.

"Pulque," she said. "Free is the refill."

"Potent is the drink," I said, giving her five bucks. "What's in it?"

"Yes," she said, then walked away.

There was a stunning Latina woman seated alone at the bar to my left. We briefly locked eyes, and there was a connection. The spider of fate had spun a fine thread between the two of us. All I had to do was approach her, spark up a conversation, and the spider would weave his web. We'd fall in love, have eleven children, and buy a house with a spare room large enough for a proper Jesus exhibit.

I avoided eye contact at all costs, glancing around for someone to save me. Pancake was nowhere to be found. Edgar was chatting with some cowboys.

"Hola," said the woman.

"Hola," I said. "Tú eres hermosa."

She laughed at me.

I laughed too. But what was funny? She was, indeed, beautiful.

I quickly told myself that I had intentionally squandered the opportunity, that I meant to stomp on the spider. But really, I had said exactly what popped into my mind. We're far better at getting to the point in a language we barely know. In my native English tongue, I would have bombarded myself with a million possible things to say to her, grown paralyzed by the weight of saying any of them, and ended up saying nothing at all. I would just keep drinking and thinking and eventually convince myself that, if I only had the time and courage to spill my soul to her, she'd be a fool not to love me.

Pancake barged in the back door in his boxers, his hair soaking wet, holding his pants. He approached the bar, muttered something about the *microonda* to the bartender, and handed over his pants. She disappeared into the back kitchen area.

"Gotta zap those microbes," I said.

"Kaboomba," he said. "Any sign of Joey-boy?"

"No," I said. "Your Spanish is getting good though."

"Certain phrases," he said.

"¿De dónde eres?" I asked.

"Jesus only spoke Arabic," he said.

"I think it was Aramaic," I said.

He snapped his focus to a painting of Frida Kahlo on the wall and told her, "Yes, yes, I'm aware," then turned back to me. "Whatever it was, it was the Savior's only language."

"Go on," I said.

He again addressed Kahlo. "We'll get to that." Then to me: "What I'm saying is, I don't give an owl's hoot what language you speak. Little Jesús didn't speak a lick of Spanish, did he? But guess what? They're not hurting for Bibles in Tijuana."

That was all.

Pancake filled up a cup of pulque for himself, then glided over to the Frida painting to settle their differences. I dropped another five on the bar to cover him, then watched as two guys played a series of pool. The table was totally free: no charge. At Hugh Two, games cost fifty cents, which is a good deal, but the money adds up. I often spend twenty bucks a day on pool. The upside of this is that I consider every quarter a generous donation to the Hugh Two cause, a form of philanthropy. There are starving children in Africa, yes, but people are hurting here too. And we come to places like this. Altruism aside, though, you cannot beat a free pool table. This bar was a paradise. Perhaps we'd gotten Joseph A all wrong. If he hung out in places like this, he was clearly not a Joseph A. He was a street person, possibly a criminal, an upstanding citizen.

"I'm having trouble picturing Joseph A in here," I said to Pancake.

"He's a lifeguard," he said. "Place needs savin'."

"Yooooooo!" shouted someone upon entering the bar.

It was Bumper, wearing his usual uniform of a tie-dye shirt and baggy sweatpants. He shuffled over to us with a busy jaw that screamed amphetamines.

"What the hell are you guys doing here?" asked Bumper.

"Long story," I said.

"We are not compatible," said Pancake.

"Oh, come on, Pancake," fussed Bumper. "You're gunna act like this again?"

"To get along with you would be the act," said Pancake. He spotted the bartender reemerging with his microwaved pants, giving him an opportunity to exit the conversation, which he would have done either way.

"I don't know what his deal is," said Bumper. "I'm nothing but nice to him."

"The fly thing," I said.

"He's still pissed about that?"

I nodded.

A year or so prior, a fly landed on Bumper's shoulder at Hugh Two, and he killed it. Pancake witnessed the murder and retaliated, smacking Bumper across the back with a pool cue. That event was the initial source of Pancake's animosity, but over time he has developed a more general hatred of Bumper. While I'm by no means a fan of Bumper myself, I have unfortunately grown to put up with him.

One thing you must understand about cocaine people is that they're never going to stop showing up. You can tell them you detest them, but they'll be back the next day hell-bent on changing your mind. You are great, the cocaine tells them. The world will see it eventually. When it comes to cocaine people, the choice is either to entirely avoid them or learn to endure them. Given Bumper's affection for Hugh Two, full avoidance was impossible.

"How you been, man?" asked Bumper. "You doing good? You look good." He started rubbing my shoulders and patting my back and doing cocaine things. "You're doing well, aren't you? You're killing it."

"I'm alright," I said.

"How's the book coming along? You're crushing it, aren't you? You fucking beast. I can't wait to read it. It's going to be big, man. Colossal."

During a previous blackout, I had opened up to Bumper about my aspirations to write a book. It was an egregious mistake, and I do believe cocaine was involved.

"I'm still plotting it out," I lied.

"You'll nail it down."

"Hopefully."

"One hundred percent," said Bumper. He put a supportive arm around me. The cocaine didn't just have him confident in himself tonight. He was confident in me. A preposterous gamble.

One of the caballeros waved to Bumper.

"That's my guy," said Bumper.

"Oh, I see," I said, connecting the dots as to why Bumper would come to such a place.

"He's got the good shit," said Bumper. "These guys get it straight from Colombia. This is your first time here, I assume?"

I nodded.

"This place is a riot," he said. "I come for the blow, but I stay for the fiesta. It gets rowdy in here. These Hispanics, they know how to have a good time. When it gets real late, they clear these tables out and dance and there's always piñatas and free soda and shit. I don't know if it's always someone's birthday or something, but I'm down. Who doesn't love a piñata?" He continued, but I tuned out his voice.

I wasn't sure where I fit into the discussion. When Pancake talks to himself, at least there's no victim. Bumper attacks you. It's criminal. But that's cocaine: Do enough of it, and you are the conversation. You are the questions and the answers, the alpha and the omega. I am no stranger to cocaine myself. I had a brief addiction in my mid-twenties. But I was never one to trap someone in a conversation and tell him how his dreams would play out. I would just snort lines in my living room and have so much internal dialogue going on that a real-life conversation didn't stand a chance.

Cocaine seems to make most people optimists. It has never worked that way for me. The minute it enters my bloodstream, I become a strict realist. I see my craziest dreams as just that: crazy. And as I listened to Bumper rant, I caught a secondhand high. There I stood depressed and drunk in a crumbling bar, hoping in the back of my mind that I would somehow write a book. And not just any book. I'm talking about a good book, something dark and insightful, a handbook for the damned. That's nice, whispered reality. Good luck with that. You'll need it.

"Isn't that the chef from Hugh Two?" asked Bumper.

"Yeah, that's Edgar."

"Edgar, yea," said Bumper. "I love that guy." He waved to a confused Edgar, who gestured for me to join him.

I slipped away, meeting Edgar in the cramped bathroom, the lights flickering. There was a small figurine of Our Lady of Guadalupe glued to the back of the toilet.

"What's up?" I asked.

"That man," said Edgar.

"Bumper," I said.

"He's the plague," said Pancake, straining on the toilet in the doorless stall.

"He is the one, yes?" asked Edgar.

"Which one?" I asked Edgar.

"The man with the collars on his shirt," said Edgar. "Mr. Joseph A."

"Wait, are you saying collars? Or colors?"

"Verde, blue, yellow," said Edgar. "Collars."

I chugged my cup of sweet death.

HANGOVERS

I try not to run from the morning-after darkness, the agony. Some people prefer to down ten drinks and race back to intoxication. But the key is to walk away from the sadness at a steady pace, like a crime boss being tailed by the cops. They don't slam on the gas and leave the authorities in the dust. They drive with purpose, they make clever turns, they strategically accelerate through yellow lights. Because they know it's all part of the life. They signed up for this. It's a waste of energy to sprint away from the hurt when it'll be back tomorrow. Such is the natural condition of things. There are actions and reactions, there are chickens and eggs, there are drinks and sorrows....

Chapter 5

*If you can see your path laid out in front of you step by step,
you know it's not your path.*
—Joseph Campbell

The hangover was all-world.

My brain was clawing at my skull: anywhere but here. And my mouth, it was beyond dry, like I was chewing on textiles. This was in fact the Battle of Thermopylae. The sun up there, that's Adolf Hitler. That lawnmower down the block is Joseph Stalin. Enemies are everywhere. We're in the thick of it now, gentlemen. This is a battle for the free world. They'll talk about us for generations. They'll sing songs about us.

Sometimes the most gruesome of hangovers must be framed like this. The mornings are warfare. And you have no right to complain about being in the trenches. You drafted yourself.

I somehow made it to the dining room table, to the rum. I had slept right through the precious morning. Everything beyond the window was aglow, fending off the rays. Looming up in that sky was the midday sun. I could feel its judgment. It was looking down at me, scrutinizing, shaking its head. The rest of the bluebirds were up at sunrise. What's your excuse?

I apologize, my fellow bluebirds.

This happens sometimes.

The drinks win.

You should be thankful, dear bluebirds, that you are a sober species, for the hangover is the devil. Under such conditions, consciousness is simply not an option. I had to sleep through it. Sleep is wonderful, is it not? There's nothing like a good stint in the nest. A long and dreamless sleep, a brush with beautiful nonexistence.

Nothing was good enough to be liked on this particular morning. I did not like myself. I did not like this drink. I did not like the clinking ice. I did not like the fact that I had to put in a momentous effort to lift the cup to my mouth. The pain of sitting reminded me of my time in an office, in the fluorescent sadness. So much agony, so much sitting. At least in this chair I have an honorable and definite goal. This bottle, it's only so big. And when it goes dry, the mission isn't over. I must drink the remaining bottles in the house, I must go to Port Liquor, I must buy more bottles identical to this one, I must return to the dining room table.

Most will disagree with my objectives, but you can't deny my resolve. There are tasks, and they get completed. At your average job, half the effort is put toward creating the illusion of effort. That's not the case here. I am doing things. I am pure productivity, a child of Adam Smith. My life is free enterprise: a conscious consumer who takes a fifteen-minute walk, exchanges his capital for goods, then labors over a bottle. I only purchase a few bottles at a time because it maintains this discipline, this balance, this microeconomic cycle.

* * *

"Mr. John," I said as I strolled into Hugh Two.

"The good boy," said Mr. John, patting me on the back. "Do you have something to smoke for me?"

I gave him a smoke and lit one for myself. We stood in foggy silence for a few minutes as he studied my face. He occasionally nodded to himself as if reading my history, matching up every blunder of my life to its corresponding wrinkle.

"It is a hard day," said Mr. John.

I nodded.

"I used to make the copy of the key," he said.

"What key?"

"My job," he said, his eyes lowering in shame. "Home Depot. I make the copy of the key for the customers."

I patted his back in return. With a gig like that, he was well-acquainted with sorrow.

Gigi must have seen me chatting with Mr. John and known by my face that it was no time for lollygagging. I was here on business. When I collapsed into the stool, a rummy-boy was waiting for me. It was like the first breath after being held under water for a few years.

Pancake plopped down beside me. I could smell the meth exhaust on his red and black flannel. He leaned forward and, upon seeing my face, said, "Holy marlin."

"Yeah," I said.

"Roger," he said, saluting me and disappearing.

Everyone in the bar could tell I was in a bad place.

Gigi kept the drinks coming.

Penny stuck to soft, somber tunes on the jukebox, mostly early Frankie Miller and some Nick Drake. She had her baby nephew with her, but when he'd start crying, she took him out to the back alley to spare me the noise. Leave him out in the Beauty, I suggested.

Pancake maintained distance.

Mr. John slept in his chair.

Lana rubbed my back, nodding out as she did so.

Edgar brought me a cup of pickle juice from the kitchen. I barely kept it down.

I was a patient among world-class doctors. The hurt know the hurt.

"Are you feeling up to it today?" asked Gigi.

"No," I said.

"Oh, because it's just that terrible, huh?"

"Probably."

"You'll come around."

"I doubt it."

"I believe in you," she said.

"What are we referring to?" I asked.

She pointed the soda gun at me and walked away.

I stared at myself in the shattered mirror behind the bar. That mirror makes sense, I thought. That mirror is like all of us. In it we see a perfect reflection of ourselves, comfortably fucked up individuals, our souls shattered into a million pieces, some parts permanently missing, stolen by some stranger turned lover turned stranger again.

Down the bar, Penny let out a long, anguished exhale as she scratched another scratch-off ticket. According to myth, about six years ago Penny won $1,300 on a scratcher. She talks about it as though she won a billion dollars. That one victory has kept her scratching ever since. On average, she scratches about twenty tickets a day. She'll win the occasional five bucks here and there, but for the most part she loses, throws the ticket onto the filthy floor, and waits for Mr. John to retrieve the ticket and double check the numbers. This was exactly what she was doing today, but Mr. John was asleep. Hoping to wake him up, Penny threw popcorn at him, but he was in a heavy slumber. Eventually she gave up.

A group of four middle-aged women, all of them below average-looking, came wandering into the bar at one point. It was a bachelorette party. The drunkest among them wore a purple sash: *OFF THE MARKET SOON.*

Pancake cornered the pack and began lecturing them about the institution of marriage. It was fraudulent, he warned them. Get out while you still can, ladies. Traditional matrimony exists for the sole purpose of perpetuating the power of feudal lords.

Surprisingly, the women agreed. The bride-to-be openly admitted that she was very much participating in said system, marrying a commercial real estate tycoon for his money and status. This was a source of bonding between her and Pancake, and Pancake hugged her. The women were very fond of him, treating him as a kind of gentle animal. Each of them hugged him one by one. Then, as the fourth woman embraced Pancake, he squeezed the poor woman's ass. But she seamlessly returned the favor, smacking his ass in return. Pancake was authentically disappointed that she had handled it with such grace, because his intention was to cause a ruckus and perhaps be smacked across the face. He wanted to let these women know that, while the whole group might be in agreement about the corruption of the marital institution, he was not to be considered tamed and predictable. He was a heathen, liable to go rogue even on his own kin. Eventually he threatened to kill the bride-to-be's husband if they didn't leave the bar and never come back.

After ten or so drinks I started to feel okay again, so I made my way over to the claw machine to give Camilla some attention. One of the stuffed animals trapped inside the machine, a purple elephant, has long been the target of attempted rescue missions. Her name is Camilla. It's unclear why she became the only important creature in the tank. Like most of the traditions of Hugh Two, it just happened one night and the next day it was the law of the land.

I donated two quarters to the cause, then pushed the START button. On came the claw machine's hopeful little jingle. Up went the claw. I steered it into position. Down it went.

I failed.

Pancake came barging in from the back alley and was ecstatic to see that I was on my feet and over the hump, therefore eligible for conversation: "I'm closing in on Joey Boy."

"Oh yeah?"

"Oh yeah," he said.

"You're really turning the city upside down."

"No turn unstoned," he said. "Joey-boy lives in the vicinity of Pine and Broadway."

"Shocker," I said.

"The belly of the beast," he said. "Pure wealth." He played a drum roll on the bar, put his hands to his mouth, and announced to the bar, "Rich people are communists!"

Only I was listening. "Go on," I told him.

"The richer you are," he said, "the more you might think you're a capitalist. But really, you're a Commie, a Joseph A, a goddamn robot." He stopped to ponder, nodding to himself, an idea coming to him. "More like a Joseph S, if you catch my drifter." Proud of the Stalin reference, he gave himself a handshake. "They say capitalism is about the individual, about freedom, do they not?"

I nodded.

"Then why does everyone and their fucking mother look the same out there?" He pointed to the door as if there were two worlds: Hugh Two and everywhere else. "They go on their precious internet, they shop at the same places, they listen to the same fucking songs. They're the goddamn tide, up and down, up and down, and money's the moon." He howled, likely because the moon reminded him of werewolves. "Each and every rich fuck out there is lookin' to throw their money at the brightest light in the highest tower. And it doesn't matter if you sell 'em handbags or shoes or mansions or fucking cheesesteaks: It's about the price being high, and not the product itself. As long as the price is high, they'll show. Oh, they'll show, baby, like fleas to a street kitty. And is that any way to be an individual? No, no, it's not. The people with no money at all, we're the real individuals, the free thinkers. You've gotta think good and hard about how to spend your money when you've got none."

"You're onto something," I said.

"Of course I am."

"Why cheesesteaks though?"

"No, just cheese," he said. "Fancy cheese, like on a serving board: hors d'oeuvres."

"But you said cheesesteaks."

"Aristocrats like steaks too," he said.

"Okay, but—"

"Whose fucking side are you on?!" he snapped.

"Yours."

"Good," he said. "We've got work to do."

He scurried over to the pool table and fetched his garbage bags from beneath it. If he's not rolling around with his shopping cart, Pancake always carries two garbage bags of belongings, even if he only has a few items. This way he can balance them over his left shoulder, one draped behind him, one in front. He did this with his bags as he returned to my side. I could see the outline of a few bean cans in the front bag.

He reached into the bag and pulled out a can. The loss of weight threw off the garbage bag equilibrium, sending the back bag toward the floor, but Pancake quickly snatched the whole apparatus before it could slip out of place. His reflexes are naturally phenomenal, but they're world-class when he's blasted on meth. He grabbed a few of Penny's empty Budweiser's and dropped them into the front bag, restoring balance to the system. Then he sliced open a can of baked beans with his switchblade. It would take a civilian ten minutes to do this. It takes Pancake five seconds.

He drank some beans.

"Today's the day!" he sang in baritone. "That Joey-boy comes out to play!" He tooted an imaginary trumpet, then got back to the lyrics. "We will find him..." He fumbled for words, briefly hesitating, then sorted out a rhyme to his song. "And he will pay!" He was very disappointed in himself for faltering lyrically. He dropped his head and took off toward the door, berating himself under his breath. On his way out, he punched a hole in the wall and muttered, "Wasted opportunity..."

This woke up Mr. John.

* * *

Amir kicked us out of Port Liquor after Pancake stole a few items.

I stood at the locked door. "I just need a bag of ice."

"The ice is for him, I know," he said, gesturing to Pancake. "For his satchels, where he keeps the stolen things. It's in the satchels, I tell you. You check for yourself."

"Yes, but it's for my drink too."

"The stolen things, he must return them."

"To dust you shall return!" shouted Pancake.

I negotiated an exchange between the enemy parties.

Pancake slowly conceded more and more stolen goods. First came a few bananas, then ice cream, then a pair of those cloth gloves with grippy dots on them, then four sodas, a dustpan, and a donut. Amir knew exactly what items were taken because he simply watched Pancake steal them. There was a long fight over the dustpan accusation. I pointed out to Pancake that the outline of a dustpan was clearly visible through his front garbage bag. He claimed the outline was actually a rare type of plunger that he had bartered for a few miles back. As this was clearly false, I paid for the dustpan to appease Amir.

"Do not return," said Amir.

Pancake and I set up shop on the corner of Joseph A's supposed residence. We sat on the curb drinking and waiting, with Pancake accusing anyone in the area of being in cahoots with Joseph A. There were four potential apartment buildings that Joey may have lived in, all of which were modern and shiny and well-kept. By societal standards, it was perhaps the nicest intersection in Downtown Long Beach.

Our stakeout went on well into the night. After four hours, I suggested we head back to Hugh Two, but Pancake vehemently resisted. He said with confidence that Joey will *showy* and hinted that I too might be a Joseph A co-conspirator, threatening to strike me with the dustpan. I told him I'd never seen a plunger that looked like that.

At one point, a group of nuns strolled by, and we harassed them. Initially we taunted them because of their funny outfits, but once they were gone, the discussion took a religious turn. Pancake and I went down a wormhole about how God is likely dealing with the worst case of PTSD in history. Even if heaven is the coziest, most utopian location in the universe, the Lord has still had to watch us humans, his precious children, do all of the hideous things we've done: perpetual wars, Genghis Khan pillaging and raping the planet, slavery, reality television, the European destruction of the Americas, social media, Ernest Hemingway, atomic bombs, the Holocaust.

Pancake and I concurred that, if God ever did exist, there was a strong chance he'd committed suicide by now. If humanity hadn't pushed him to the edge yet, he must be a very strong man, said Pancake. Yes, I agreed, perhaps even a god. But I can only hope that the modern world has him considering a move in the apocalyptic direction, because if his billions of offspring mainlining the internet and burning the planet into a smoldering rock doesn't have him at least thinking about snapping his fingers and ending this little experiment, he's no god in my book.

Eventually I ran out of rum.

I do believe more was purchased.

* * *

The house smells of lasagna.

As Nanna shuffles about in the kitchen, the stairs creak beneath Poppy's feet as he comes down with a book in his hand.

"This is the one," he says.

"Who is it?" I ask.

"One of my favorites," he says, slowly making his way across the dining room. He sets the book before me on the table: *Fear and Trembling* by Søren Kierkegaard. I examine the minimalist gray and white cover, the tattered spine, the yellowed pages.

"What's the gist of it?" I ask.

"There is no gist," he says.

"Never ask your grandfather for a summary," says Nanna, entering from the kitchen with the lasagna. "He's against saving time."

"I'm against anything that doesn't stick," says Poppy, immediately sampling the lasagna.

"That's why he never cooks," says Nanna. "Food is too fleeting. There's no lessons hidden in the cheese here, no timeless truth in the act of stuffing your face."

Our laughter conquers the room, then becomes a warm and cozy quiet.

"While you were sitting here and Nanna was in the kitchen cooking," says Poppy. "Did you know it was lasagna?"

"It's always lasagna," I say.

"Hey," says Nanna.

"The best lasagna on the planet," I say.

"In the universe," says Nanna.

"Let's not jump to conclusions," says Poppy. "If there's life out there, they may be damn good in the kitchen. Why would you assume we're the only culinary species?"

"He can never just give me anything," says Nanna. "Always ruining the party with logic."

"Let's say you'd never met Nanna," says Poppy. "Would you have known what she was cooking in there?"

"Yeah," I say. "I can smell it."

"Bingo," says Poppy. "You can smell it. And would you like it if you could only smell it? If I made you smell this lasagna only to prevent you from actually tasting it?"

"Poppy's torture chamber," says Nanna.

"Of course not," I say.

"Well, that's what a gist is," says Poppy. "You never want the gist."

"If the book is as old as this one seems," I say. "I might want the gist."

"1843," says Poppy. "And what does age have to do with it?"

"He's worried it's outdated and boring," says Nanna. "Like us."

"Those are your words, not mine," I say.

"The world doesn't have a gist," says Poppy.

"The real question is," says Nanna. "Is my lasagna good before you taste it? Or is it only in the act of tasting it that it becomes good."

"The chicken and the egg," says Poppy.

NAMES

Most people find it awkward to forget someone's name. They'll avoid talking to a person for fear of having to admit it. To me, this is a strange phenomenon. Names are of little importance. It's your story that I'm after. And if it turns out that your story isn't worth my time, if I know everything you've done and everything you're going to say because your opinions are regurgitated and you have no taste for chaos, that's the real awkwardness for me. I could know your name, your birth date, and your social security number, but I will avoid you at all costs, even if we're the only two people in the room. I'll awkwardly exit the conversation, head out into the alley, and smoke as many cigarettes as it takes to escape. Meanwhile, I have no problem mingling with complete strangers without ever asking their names. Introductions are a waste of time if both parties recognize each other as quality. Some of the finest things I've ever heard have been uttered by strangers in dark rooms, people whose words stood alone like monuments. I never did get their names....

Chapter 6

I rebel; therefore we exist.
—Albert Camus

It was the early morning, still dark.

The ginger ale had gone dry, so I mixed my rum with expired orange juice. I myself don't trust expiration dates. They're a scam intended to churn the wheels of capitalism. Nonetheless, this juice was indeed expired. I wasn't even sure how it got into the refrigerator. Poppy used to drink OJ, so it must have been in there since his passing. It was antique orange juice, aged and acidic. But it did well for its age. It got the job done. After all, rum is a star. It needs only a little support, by means of transportation, the other ingredients being a kind of tour bus. The almighty rum must board the bus, then it's escorted down the esophagus and dropped off in the stomach. It's just a matter of metabolism after that. Soon it enters the bloodstream. And before you know it, the rum is on stage, smiling and singing, and I am in the crowd to hear its happy song: Life is not so bad, the heavy things are not so heavy, suffering is funnier than success, etc.

Eventually the darkness became dawn. The desolate world beyond the murky dining room window materialized. I saw the grass. I saw the sky and the clouds. I saw the lime tree. I saw Mrs. Connolly's house. I heard the cars and planes and other machines.

And then came the bluebird.

He swooped down and came to a graceful perch on the outside windowsill. Sitting there silently, his head darted back and forth, surveying, judging the world, objective and aware. I wish I knew you were coming, bluebird. I would have left the window open for you. I would have poured you a drink. I would have—

He turned directly toward me. Our eyes locked.

Yes, yes, I knew you heard me, old friend.

You recognize me, don't you?

We have squawked together many times.

My call is your call, my blood your blood.

Is it me you are seeing?

Or do you see only your reflection in the windowpane?

It doesn't matter.

Whether you see you or you see me, you see a bluebird.

We are so righteous, you and I.

Because we know what we are.

It will soon be time to squawk together.

That is what we do, we squawk and squawk until we wake up all of them, every other creature, the cats and dogs and the flowers and trees and the insects and humans and anything else stupid enough to keep existing.

Rise and shine, bastards.

Welcome to The Ruthless Now.

And so, we squawked. We squawked and we squawked. Time dissolved. It seemed to me that I disappeared for a while. I flew away. But when I returned, there I was, sitting at the dining room table. My friend was gone. The world had been awoken.

We've come a long way, the bluebirds and I. At one time we were adversaries. Every damn sunrise they'd screech away in the garden, destroying my sleep, giddily getting their precious days started. For a while, my first glimpse of daylight was a glare off the tops of their heads, a white speck glinting off blue feathers, a caustic daily reminder that unfortunately our solar system's source of warmth and life hadn't burned out while I was semi-consciously gasping for air for six hours.

I so desperately wanted to know the genus and species of these birds so I could hate them by their full name. But by the time I got out of bed they were always gone. So I long settled for hating those fucking birds in the window.

Things changed, though, when I gave up on sleep. These days I do still end up horizontal each night for a few hours—a gallon of rum will do that—but I've abandoned the traditional routine of eight hours. A human needs eight hours of sleep, that's what I've been told since I was a child. But that claim turned out to be just as baseless as all the other norms people accept for themselves. You have to figure out what works for you. And not the you of the past or the you you're hoping to be. I'm referring to the you of the now. Most people are not well-acquainted with this person. But I am. And what works for me right now is forgoing sleep, thus evading hangovers, and spending my extra time drinking and thinking and being a bluebird at the dining room table.

The hangovers were the real problem. Once I got rid of them, that's when I became curious about the bluebirds. They are beautiful birds, elegant and sleek. And the more I listened to their squawking, the more it seemed to be a kind of beckoning to me. So, I did some research on the internet. There are so many birds on this planet. Tens of thousands of species. After an hour of scrolling, I arrived at the rather obvious conclusion that the blue birds in the window are bluebirds. I admire the biologist who decided on that name, because whoever it was had an appreciation for straightforwardness. No grand labels or wordy descriptions of beak shape.

It's a fucking bird. It's blue.

A bluebird.

Their call is wonderful, really. It's repetitive, yes—basically the same shriek over and over—but it's perfectly fitting. A bird that's blue and makes only one sound. There's no confusion about what we're dealing with here. That's how I came to be a bluebird, why they consider me blood. With me, what you see is what you get. I know who I am. I don't waste my life away trying to become someone else.

There was a knock at the door.

At first, I figured it was Mrs. Connolly coming over to complain about the noise. That's always an easy fix. I tell her to fuck off, and she does, but then, as she walks back to her house, I tell her that I am kidding, that I will try to quiet down. But I never do. This knocking, though, it was a different type of knocking. Mrs. Connolly is a woman of class, with a gentle and friendly knock. This knock had power to it, and no cadence.

I made my way to the window and peeked through the blinds. It was Officer Nellins.

I slowly opened the door and rubbed my eyes as if he had woken me up. Immediately recognizing me, he said, "Well now," placing his hand on his baton.

"Can I help you?"

"Are you a resident of this domicile?"

"Domicile?"

"The home."

"Oh."

He craned forward, peering over my shoulder into the house.

I pulled the door closed behind me and stepped onto the porch. "What can I do for you?"

"What happened to your tent?"

"That's a vacation home."

Officer Nellins leaned within inches of my face and did a little sniffle to let me know he could smell the rum.

I chuckled.

"Is this a joke to you?" he asked.

"Is what a joke?"

"Everything."

"Almost," I said. "I'm working on it."

"Who owns the home?"

"Me," I said.

"We received a noise complaint."

"Yeah, it's the bluebirds." I gestured up into a tree. "It's mating season."

He investigated the empty tree.

"I assume Mrs. Connolly, the woman next door, she called you?"

He said nothing.

"She very well could be experiencing Alzheimer's-related cognitive decline," I said. "The build-up of amyloid plaques in her brain, possibly caused by REM sleep deprivation. That's an oversimplification of the disease though. It's still a mystery." I checked my wrist for the time as if I was wearing a watch. "Anyway, long story short, her son, Gerardillo, comes around about once a month or so to check on her, to make sure she hasn't fallen down the stairs or wandered off into traffic or something like that. Her stairs are extremely steep, way too steep for the elderly. Gerardillo is a good guy though. He's an accountant up in Sacramento, and his wife is a professor. I think she's in the sciences. But, yeah, Mrs. Connolly is always knocking on my door and asking me to quiet down as if I'm a bluebird myself. I never know what to say to the poor woman."

Officer Nellins squinted at me. My backstory was so thorough that he thought I might be telling the truth. Why would I have gone through the trouble to provide so many details, to mention Gerardillo and break down the pathology of Alzheimer's and describe the gradient of her stairs? In reality, of course, Mrs. Connolly did not have children, nor Alzheimer's. I had never seen her stairs. I had also never met a man named Gerardillo and was unsure if the name existed.

"The bluebirds," I continued, "their call is a kind of shriek. It's jarring, very jarring, so I don't blame Mrs. Connolly for calling you. I gotta get back to work though."

"And what is it that you do?" he asked condescendingly.

"I'm planning on being a writer."

"Planning?"

"Years of it."

I floated back inside and waited, keeping the door ajar as Nellins descended the porch and opened the door to his police cruiser. Timing it flawlessly, just as he ducked into the car and I was out of view, I let out the loudest bluebird call in the history of bluebirds.

"You hear that?" I asked him.

He rolled down his window and scowled at me.

"Mating season," I said.

* * *

When you're the first person to show up at the bar, some people might label you a reprobate. But I don't go to the bar early only because I need to drink. I go to witness the set-up, the work. I go to become a better person, to foster gratitude.

Gigi wipes down the counters, cuts lemons and limes, stocks the straws and coasters, ices down the coolers. In between each task, she shoots whiskey and pours me another.

Mr. John sits beside the door, dozing off into pleasant naps, occasionally jerking awake and nodding to himself as if remembering he has something to do.

Penny lifts up her shirt, jabbing herself in the belly with an insulin needle, then carefully places the used syringe, needle-down, into her empty Budweiser.

The flies patrol overhead, buzzing and circling. They land on my face and the toilet and the rim of my drink.

Edgar clanks around in the kitchen, cursing in Spanish at his television, the tang of burned buffalo wings and Marlboros riding the breeze.

It's pure administration, and it's all very sacred.

It doesn't matter if you're going to a bar or a bakery, you have to show up early every once in a while. Witnessing how something is built is crucial for respecting the overall apparatus. Kicking down an anthill becomes astronomically more difficult if you watch its construction. A million ants working in harmony, concerted effort, the beauty of nature. If you can still manage to destroy an ant domicile after watching it be built, you should be shot. Even piles of dirt and shithole bars are the brainchildren of keen organization.

"What is it this morning?" asked Gigi.

"Nothing," I said.

"It's never nothing with you."

"I'm just thinking."

"About what? Your next work of bathroom graffiti?" She downed a shot of whiskey. "Or are you pondering the fate of the universe, over-analyzing shit, driving yourself mad, that sort of thing?"

"Precisely."

"You're gunna worry yourself into the grave."

"Live fast, die middle-aged," I said.

"You'll get this drink once you tell me what you're thinking about."

"Nonsense," I said.

"Oh, I know it's nonsense," she said. "But it makes me feel better to hear you say some of the stuff you say. It makes me feel sane, you know?" She stood in front of me, holding my drink hostage. She took a sip.

"I was thinking about Tupac," I said.

"The rapper?"

"Yea, well, him and people like him," I continued. "Karl Marx, Tupac, Solzhenitsyn, those kinds of people. There are a lot better examples that I can't think of right now, but my point is, they were all uprooted from their homes in some way or another and were forced to move elsewhere. And I think people like that, who aren't stuck in one place in a physical sense, their minds get freed up, and it allows them to marry an idea. Like, if you don't have to dedicate a large part of your brain to a homeland or a tribe or a country, you can go all-in on a philosophy or a mindset. You can build a message that transcends borders and artificial identities and resonates with more people because you didn't try to anchor it to any specific geographical location."

"You're retarded," said Gigi, setting my drink down.

"I'm glad to be of assistance."

A hefty construction worker strolled in a few minutes later. He set his hardhat on the bar and plopped down beside me. As he sunk into the stool, the cushion compressed, the air escaping: a sigh of relief. I'd met the guy a handful of times before but couldn't remember his name. He nodded to me, I nodded back. A few months prior he had told me about a neighbor of his who had a habit of blasting music at 3:00am on weeknights. We had discussed potential retaliation plots.

"You end up taking action?" I asked. "With your neighbor?"

He chuckled and went on to tell me that he had slashed all four tires on his neighbor's car. But the neighbor apparently didn't get the message. The late-night music continued. So he waited for his neighbor to replace the tires, then he again slashed the tires, this time spray-painting across the windshield: *Thank You For Keeping It Down*. This was excellent, I said, and I bought him a shot of whiskey to celebrate his immaculate revenge. He drank it, washed it down with a few beers, then wished me farewell. The lunch break was over.

As he headed out the door, I heard Pancake's cart. He came in hot, swerving around my construction worker friend at full speed, somehow avoiding him and Mr. John to make a risky yet demolition-free entrance.

"Pancake, do you have to?" yelled Gigi.

"Rain," he said. Then, rolling by me, he poked me in the neck, whispering, "There are matters." He disappeared into the alley—*beep, beep, beep*—then he scurried back in and sat beside me. Right away he noticed that the stool cushion was more deflated than usual. He hopped off it, leaning down to examine its level of compression.

"The fat guy was sitting there," I explained.

"Eighteen stone," he said. "That's 250 to you, Yankee." He hopped back up onto the stool. I lit him a cigarette. He took his standard minute-long opening puff.

"What are the matters?" I asked.

"Let me get established first," he said.

Gigi brought him a double vodka. He paid in all nickels, then downed it.

"A lotta silver today," I said.

"Nickels are the redheaded stepchildren of American currency," he said.

"Hear! Hear!" he shouted British Parliament-style.

"Let the man speak!" he rallied for himself.

"I stole a tip jar," he muttered to me. "Denny's over on Sixth." Suddenly he started to tremble. He took three deep breaths and gripped the bar. His arms tensed. His temples quivered. The whole bar began to shake like it was one of his limbs.

"Pancake, please," said Gigi.

Pancake released his death grip and rotated to face me. "I was over in Joey A's neck of the woods, doing laps."

"Laps?" I asked.

"Surveillance," he said. "I'm circling the block, circling, circling..." He started slowly spinning around in his stool, continuing as he rotated: "I ran recon for a while, then last night, just like I knew he would, Joey-boy showed."

"Did you confront him?" I asked.

"Well, that's the thing," said Pancake.

"What's the thing?" I asked.

"Contingencies emerged," said Pancake. He leaned over the bar, grabbed a pen, and started drawing on a napkin. Nothing about his depiction correlated even slightly to what he said: "He walks up this way, down Pine, and I trail him. I thought he was going to go in this shop, the one with the red awning on the corner, but then he goes into this building, so I tail him, I tail him good, like a breeze on wind."

Gigi brought him another vodka. He drank it, then smashed the glass on the floor.

"Pancake!" screamed Gigi.

"The bastard!" yelled Pancake.

"You better cut the shit!" yelled Gigi.

Pancake kicked the bar. *Crunch!* His foot went through the rotting wood. Gigi pointed the soda hose at him. "Do you want to get cut off?!"

Pancake let out a wolf's howl. At first it was visceral and threatening, but over the course of ten seconds it faded into regret and apology. He dropped his head and tried to rotate his stool away from Gigi as a means of accepting his mistake, but his foot was stuck in the bar.

Mr. John arrived with his broom. "Bad man, bad man, bad man..." he muttered, sweeping the broken glass into a pile under the pool table. He placed a coaster atop the remnants—his form of a caution sign—then went back out front.

By the time I dislodged Pancake's foot from the bar, he had forgiven himself. He lit another cigarette and hovered over his incoherent napkin diagram: "He goes into this building, so I sneak up behind him to make my entrance." He sipped my drink, some ashes falling into it, then leaned back in his chair to deliver the big news. "But the door, it had a lock."

"Every building has a lock," I said.

"This one too," he said.

* * *

Pancake and I were three games into a heated series: a race to five. I was down 2-1. But the pool table kept stealing my quarters. Every game Pancake slid two quarters into the slots, but the table wouldn't register the payment. It wasn't until we donated another fifty cents that the balls would drop and the game could begin. We tried all the dependable methods of repair: We blamed Gigi, we kicked the table, we cursed at it, we fed one piece of popcorn into each of the six pockets as a tribute to the billiards gods. None of it worked.

So be it. On to game four.

As I lined up to break, Pancake gestured toward the back of the bar, a military-style hand motion. Then he beelined into the bathroom. I assumed that he'd been communicating with himself, leading the Tet Offensive within his mind, so I took my shot and waited. But he didn't return. Eventually I went to check on him. He was seated on the toilet waiting for me.

"I've got a maneuver," he explained.

"We've got a series going on," I said.

"It's all a series," he said.

He instructed me to close out my tab with Gigi and exit the front door as if I was headed home. Then I was to do a lap around the block and meet him in the back alley. I did just that. When I arrived in the alley, Pancake was seated on a milk crate, an empty one set up across from him. I took a seat. His eyes rising to meet mine, he pulled two dollars in quarters from his pocket and shook them like dice.

"These are yours," he confessed. "The table's a straight shooter. I'm the crook."

"That's okay," I said.

"Of course it is," he said. "I needed to get this thing off the ground."

"What's your play?" I asked.

"I need a pack of smokes," he said.

I offered to buy him a pack.

"No, no, no," he said. "This is something I've been thinking about for a few hundred miles now, an experiment. Have you ever heard of these folks who trade for things on the..." He hesitated, ashamed that he was even about to mention the internet. "...on the world wide web? They barter with each other, like a flea market, but it's on the computers."

I nodded.

"The idea is that you start off with something small, then you trade your way up to something big. At first you have a few dollars, but you flip it, you zip it, you crack it and whip it, and you end up with something much more, something you would've never dreamed of when you first got into the game."

"Cigarettes," I said.

"Cigarettes," he said.

He broke down his plan: He would go inside and find someone else to play pool with him. He would use the money he stole from me to pay for the first game out of the kindness of his heart. Then, after winning that opening game, he would play the same trick on a new victim, embezzling quarters game after game. Once he got up to four bucks in change, he would trade it in with Gigi for cash. During this exchange, he would intentionally drop the quarters over the bar. They would scatter everywhere. There was no way Gigi would hunt down every last coin, Pancake was confident of this. She'd have to take his word for it. And he would tell her that he was owed *six dollars cold hard cash.*

"This scheme is pretty similar to Wall Street," I said.

"Wealth," said Pancake.

"She has borrowed a large sum of money from me!" he shouted, going for a German accent, I believe.

"Most of the people on Wall Street don't actually do anything," I continued. "They just move money from one place to another and take a cut. And the cut is paid to them by rich fucks who swindled the cash themselves, people who inherited money or sheltered it from taxes or created some bullshit business that stole one dollar from a hundred million different customers and employees. The clients have an excess of money to begin with, therefore they don't mind paying a cut to the boys on Wall Street if it means their money'll keep growing. Everyone wins. The only losers are the ones not playing the game."

"Rain," said Pancake. "And we're about to do some playing."

"So you're up to six dollars," I said. "Then what?"

"Cash out, score a pack of gaspers," he said. "Smokey Robinson."

"A pack is ten bucks," I said.

This was shocking news to Pancake. He hadn't bought his own pack in years. "Inflation," he said, contemplating. Eventually the answer arrived: "I'll need you for another four Georges when the time comes."

I agreed to spot him some more cash.

Might as well pay my cut.

It's an honor to play the game.

HUMANS

The human species is indeed a kind of reptile. Snakes and lizards, they shed their skin. Mankind sheds plastic and chemicals, carbon and death. Who invited us to this planet? What purpose do we serve? The dawn of man is a funny one: It is both a prerequisite for the pondering of God's existence and the nail in the coffin of that very possibility....

Chapter 7

The water was a greenish brown.

I noticed that if I oriented myself properly and squinted in a certain way, I could make the L.A. River look like a real river. All I had to do was block off my right periphery, thus erasing the graffiti-covered overpass, and half-shut my eyelids so that the far edge of the river became the end of the world and not the start of a thirty-foot concrete embankment.

I'd finally taken Pancake up on an invite to go fishing. I'd passed many times because they always go at sunrise, which sounded like work. But Pancake promised me we could drink while we fished and that Lana was a seasoned fisherman who would handle most of the effort. That sold me. I took off at sunrise and met them near the 710 freeway.

A man named Gerson—he appeared Hispanic, but Pancake kept calling him a Jew—gave us a ride north in exchange for four dollars and a bag of clementines. The entire drive up, as Lana and I sat in the trunk of his house, a 1993 Ford Explorer, Gerson and Pancake discussed how potholes are strategically created by the Department of Transportation and only repaired once they've caused a suitable amount of damage to vehicles, thus pumping money into the automotive sector. Their thesis lacked evidence, but there were indeed plenty of potholes on the journey. I spilled a lot of rum.

Once we arrived at the fishing spot, it became clear that Lana did in fact know what she was doing. She was rigging up the rods, moving elegantly, tying knots and looping shit, occasionally instructing Pancake to grab supplies from her tackle box. I was glad someone knew what they were doing, because it wasn't going to be me. I had come for the entertainment and the promise of no work.

I squinted at the river.

That's when I noticed all of the floating things. I knew the L.A. River was vile, but I'd never taken real time to admire it. A Coke bottle, a jug of motor oil, a sandal, Bud Light cans, hairspray, a brown boot, a bag of lollipops, an Amazon package, a box of plastic silverware, a tennis ball, a balloon with some kind of Disney princess on it, a waffle, a pair of jeans, a million plastic straws, a Dodgers hat, a bike tire, a billion cigarette butts.

Every once in a while, something natural like a palm tree fragment drifted by, and I felt an urge to save it, to pluck it from the sewage and cradle it in my arms and remind it that none of this was its fault. It's me who belonged out there.

"What kind of fish are we going for?" I asked.

"Carp," said Lana, baiting a hook with what looked like a red gumdrop.

"Bass," said Pancake. "Bass-o-lass."

Lana handed me a rod. "Anything we can get, really. You can eat most of what you catch. Tilapia, catfish, sunfish."

"F-105 Thunderchiefs," said Pancake.

"Is that a type of airplane?" I asked.

"Rain," he said.

Lana cast a line. I could tell instantly, by her form, that she was a specialist. I asked about our bait, apparently called boilies, and she explained that she'd handmade them on a propane skillet with eggs, cornflakes, and some other ingredients.

So we fished.

I was astonished by how many sea creatures were living beneath the flow of garbage. Occasionally a fish would leap out of the water, do a little shimmy mid-air, then slap the surface, disappearing back into the liquid landfill. It was either a taunt or a cry for help. Or perhaps they were just having fun. I read somewhere that dolphins actually fuck for the sheer pleasure of it. I wonder what marine biologist got them to admit it.

Pancake hooked a small sunfish. Lana caught a carp that could feed a family of five.

After a while, my time came. I hooked a monster. I tugged and tugged, my heart racing, but I stopped when I heard Pancake and Lana laughing at me.

"It's not a fish," said Lana.

Pancake ventured into the river, unsnagged my line, and lifted a parking cone above his head. "Union fish!" he shouted.

We laughed and drank, drank and fished.

To them, this was a fun morning. It was business as usual, survival. But I was having a major crisis, only half of which I immediately understood. This facet of it was certain: Lana's expertise crushed me. With every passing minute, it became more clear that she was a fishing savant. She dispensed advice, untangled our lines, and displayed an overall poise that spoke to experience. She had put dedication into this, probably years. I wanted so badly to be impressed by her, because she was objectively impressive.

But I made it about me.

I was mortified. Here was a homeless woman who'd mastered a craft, a true aficionado. And there I was, an expert at nothing except drinking rum and complaining about a broken world I was hellbent on not fixing.

At one point, Pancake started fishing in a more flyfishing style. He repeatedly cast and yanked his line over a specific area of the river. I was petrified that he might be an expert too. Thankfully he was not. He reeled in a full package of hot dogs and shot Lana a glance. She nodded with approval, so he tossed the frankfurters into the tackle box. It was a keeper.

Pancake was a shockingly good understudy. He was constantly looking to Lana for guidance and approval, then actually implementing her instructions. A selfless assistant. There was an uncharacteristic normalcy about his behavior, a softness, a submissiveness. It was what regular people would call cooperation.

I'd always counted on Pancake to be more unpredictable, more barbarous, more damaged than myself. He was a benchmark for my own inadequacies. But on this day, fishing in a river of shit and polypropylene, I realized that Pancake was far more complex than I'd thought. I knew there were many versions of Pancake, but to me they were all mercurial Vietnam vets who shunned everyone, smoked meth, and took orders from no one but each other. This was a different Pancake, a man in touch with his humanity. His tenderness struck the fear of God into me.

I caught nothing but garbage. I was pitiful. I was almost expecting to hook a full handle of rum and accept it as a message from Mother Earth that I might as well go home to the dining room table and drink until I was blue in the bird.

Lana caught another huge carp, bigger than the first.

She let me hold it and, for a split second, it filled me with wonder. This was a huge fish, a legitimate miracle, another meal on the table. But the joy took off down the river when I remembered that I didn't contribute at all. If anything, I was a detriment to the team. I'd hooked a parking cone, a shopping cart, a spiral notebook, and a raincoat.

I was a disgrace.

But it wasn't until Pancake hooked a carp of his own that I decided I would never go fishing again in my life. He reeled it in, smacked it over the head with a rock, then ran through the shallows to Lana. They hugged, Pancake whispered something in her ear, then Lana said, "There's my Silver." I still didn't know what the nickname meant, but it wasn't about the meaning. It was about the gesture itself, the love. I could handle seeing love at the bar, late-night love, for even I can bring myself to love things if I've had enough to drink. But this was real love, genuine and sober and horrifying.

As I watched them walking back toward the shore holding hands, I realized it wasn't jealousy that was haunting me. I wasn't mad that no one loved me. I was mad that, if a woman could manage to, I couldn't love her back. Love seemed to be for the others. It was something over there, and I was over here, way over here, wading in a river of sewage.

Lana fried the fish on the propane skillet, battering it in flour and eggs. These fish had to be polluted, filled with toxins and mercury. I thought about declining to eat on account of my health. But then I thought about my own life. I spend much of my life poisoning myself. I might as well switch up my weapon of choice.

Lana cooked me some fish to take home, but I politely declined. I didn't need any more reminders of this excursion. Most days only deserve one lap, if that.

I drank until none of this was a problem.

Not that I can recall, at least.

THE HOMELESS

When you walk by the rows of tents on Long Beach Blvd or Seventh Street, the smell of urine overwhelms you. Even when the city clears away a homeless encampment, that urine aroma remains. It works its way into the pavement. How could I not feel bad for humans living in such conditions? I certainly do. But creeping beneath my empathy is an undeniable envy. For a select few, homelessness is a decision to live outside of a broken system. A minimum wage job? No, thank you. Rent? No, I'll stick to my tent. They've opted out of the societal game while the rest of us have become hooked on comfort. In a strange, twisted way, the homeless are becoming the closest thing modern society has to indigenous people. Globalization has chopped down the Amazon, flooded Native American reservations with casinos and cigarettes, bombarded every remote island with internet and gridded normalcy. What is left for the wild ones? Of course, there are many among the homeless who are legitimately insane. But I'm oddly jealous of them too. They've been driven mad by modernity, their feral souls incompatible with a world wrangled into submission. My own ability to maintain sanity within such a system feels like complicity. I'm in bed with the enemy. Why am I able to carry on living, drinking my rum, not going mad?....

Chapter 8

He who is unable to live in society, or who has no need because he is sufficient for himself, must be either a beast or a god.
—Aristotle

A lone bluebird was making his case.

He was competing with an array of other birds. Never in my life had I heard so many creatures in the yard. It was ear-splitting. Still half-dreaming, I made the decision that I would never leave my bed. I would lie there forever. Hopefully someone would show up with food and water once a week. If not, I would pass away in the discomfort of my own home. It was a good plan, easy to execute, something I could commit to.

Then I heard the other noises: the trucks and the motorcycles, a distant helicopter, a foghorn from the port. I opened my eyes to rocks and weeds, my face pressed against the earth. It was dawn, misty dawn, a veneer of fog fighting off the sun. Sitting up, I realized I was in the Ravine. Pancake and Lana's tent was about fifty yards away.

My first order of business was to throw stuff at the seagulls. They seemed to be the most vocal, so I fired a few rocks at them. I came close, but they were moving too fast. A few of them even saw the projectiles coming and swooped out of the way. I wanted to catch one in a net and interrogate it. What are you doing here? Isn't there a real river somewhere that you can fly off to? Did God send you here strictly to taunt me?

There were scrapes on my knees. I scanned the rest of my flesh: a cut on my right hand, a bruise on my left elbow. My left eye socket throbbed. I made my way over to the bank of the river, where the water was still, to look at my reflection. My eyelid was swollen and red. It wasn't quite a black eye yet, but it would become one. The red would turn a deep blue-black and then a greenish yellow and then it would disappear, leaving the eye healed and prepared to repeat the cycle.

A fight had certainly happened. Thankfully, the evidence told me that I had honored tradition and lost. Winning a fight brings all sorts of concerns. Did I hurt the man? Or maybe I assaulted a woman? Will I be arrested today? These are, of course, hypothetical concerns for me as I've never been victorious in combat. But I'd imagine it's quite stressful. Losing, on the other hand, comes with very little baggage. Life goes on.

Lana and Pancake weren't in the tent, but there was a bottle of vodka hidden under their mattress. I hate vodka, but any port in a storm. I began drinking it to fend off the terror. Within ten minutes, I was doing just fine, able to disregard the reality of it all.

I sat on a boulder and watched the seagulls floating and diving and yelling at each other. I regretted throwing stones at them. If I could just sit down with them and explain, they might understand.

Listen, seagulls.

You might not know this by looking at me, but I'm a bird myself.

A bluebird.

But at times, my humanity kicks in.

And to be human is quite a burden.

We must make decisions for ourselves.

I know that sounds appealing, but it's not.

A decision is not what it sounds like.

It's not a control over the future.

It's only an ownership over the past.

A past we didn't even create.

It's like being interrogated about a crime.

You feel more like a witness.

But it turns out you're the culprit.

The cops say you're guilty of possessing a controlled substance: free will.

A false accusation, undoubtedly absurd.

But you're forced to defend yourself against the Leviathan.

Explain your actions.

So that's what I'm doing now, seagull.

All of this might sound stupid, so I apologize.

That, I suppose, is my overarching point: My species is not very bright.

That's why I threw the rocks at you.

I'm sorry.

I'm only human.

I heard Pancake's cart.

He and Lana appeared atop the concrete embankment. Pancake rode his cart full speed down the decline. I anticipated a violent crash, but he dropped his feet to the pavement at the last second to slow himself and gently rolled onto the grassy riverbank. Not seeing me, he disappeared into the tent for a moment.

"Good morning," I said to Lana.

"Morning," she said. "Did you sleep okay?"

"My eyes were shut," I said.

She leaned down and examined my legs. "You poor thing," she said.

I hadn't noticed: My legs were covered in mosquito bites.

"I tried to give you a sleeping bag," said Lana. "You refused."

"He hath risen," said Pancake, exiting the tent.

"I hath risen," I said. "Who did I fight?"

"That's above my pay grade, Sarge," said Pancake.

Lana didn't know either.

"They've got the Second Coming all wrong, you know," said Pancake.

"Wrong, wrong, wrong!" he sang to the sky, his voice bouncing off the nearby overpass, sending a flock of pigeons into flight.

"If Jesus is coming back here," continued Pancake, "it's not for the Second Coming. It won't be some sort of final Judgment Day. It'll just be a sequel, to take another swing at it. Christ is back, doing another lap, here to finish the job."

"What job?" asked Lana.

"Saving the world," said Pancake.

"If God's smart, he won't even send Jesus," I said. "The guy had his shot."

"This is true," said Pancake. "But nepotism goes a long way."

"Daddy owns the world," said Lana.

"He's a cosmological trust fund baby," I said.

Pancake and Lana both appreciated my comment, which I had expected. It was a good line of thought, one that had come to me months prior in the Hugh Two bathroom. I had been dying to explain it to someone, so I seized the opportunity to expound upon it. It went something like this: People say Jesus died for the world, but did the guy really have it that bad? His father set him up for success. He was popular. He had loyal minions. He had magical powers. He achieved worldwide fame. The whole thing reeks of favoritism. Sure, the man was crucified, he experienced terrible earthly agony, I'll grant him that. But who hasn't? Welcome to the club.

For the story of Jesus to be one of true sacrifice, the whole story would have to be reversed. The Son of God should be the antithesis of Jesus, a bad Jesus, a kind of problem child destined for hell. The lessons and themes would remain the same, but instead of Jesus being the example of what to do, an archetype, he would be the example of what not to do, more along the vein of Icarus. Don't be like Jesus. He steals, he kills, he fucks his neighbor's wife. He is a man riddled with flaws, perhaps addicted to alcohol and drugs, who has no career path and disappoints his father. Such would be a legitimate story of sacrifice, for God would have to deal with the disappointment that so many human fathers face: My son is a lost cause. He's bound for hell. I'll never see him again. God had it absurdly easy as a parent. Oh, your kid happened to be a gentle and loving prophet, the savior of the world? That's rather convenient. Why don't you come down here and try raising an actual human child? They're animals, not to be contained. It's a nightmare.

When keenly analyzed, the story of Jesus is not even close to a story of sacrifice. It's the story of a child blessed beyond belief who dies like the rest of us, hibernates in a cave for three days (something I would pay money to do), then ascends right back up to his father's palace. Tell me, where is the sacrifice? It seems to me that the human race is the sacrifice. We're God's hired staff, the extras, a mere backdrop for the fairytale of Jesus. They're warming up the furnaces of hell for us right now. And guess who won't be joining us down there?

Pancake loved my lecture. He clapped for a while. Lana eventually had to grab his hands and forcefully end the applause so we could resume the chat. The three of us agreed that we didn't mind Jesus. His teachings were solid. He was probably a decent guy. The only thing holding him back was that he was the son of God.

* * *

"Holler if you see the blueys," said Pancake.

I nodded.

Pancake was stealing water from a fire hydrant on Daisy and Eighth. His process was highly professional. He used a large wrench to twist off one of the caps on the side of the hydrant. Then he tightened the other two caps on the side, informing me that water can shoot out of those if you don't seal them properly. Lastly, he rotated open the top of the hydrant—the on-off lever—and out gushed cloudy water from the side of the hydrant.

"Gotta run her hard for a minute to clear out the badness," he said. He cleaned his hands and face in the flowing water, then tightened up the on-off lever slightly, easing the flow. He gazed into the gentle stream.

"The blood of the grid," he said.

I cupped some water into my hands and tasted it. It was metallic, with a rusty aftertaste, but it was water. "It's pretty good," I said.

"Municipal honey," said Pancake. He filled a five-gallon jug, then another. As he was storing them back in his cart, concealing them with a blanket, he spotted something far in the distance, down an alley. He froze in fear. "Holy marlin," he muttered to himself.

"What? Cops?" I squinted down the alley and saw a silhouetted figure a few blocks away. Whoever it was, he was merely a shadow at this distance. Pancake remained silent as the man got closer. I couldn't make out a face, but he had four dogs with him, two at each side.

"Should we run?" I backed away, plotting escape routes.

"It's no use," said Pancake. "He's seen us."

The man became less intimidating as he neared us. He was hunched and emaciated, his long beard hiding a face that was too filthy to determine his race. His dogs were grotesque Chihuahuas with dental problems abound, their teeth brown and mangled. They growled at us but went instantly silent when the man held up his hand.

"The one they call Pancake," said the man.

"Jeremiah," said Pancake.

"Helping yourself, I see," said Jeremiah.

"Just a couple fivers," said Pancake. He revealed the two jugs in his cart.

"The quantity is irrelevant," said Jeremiah. "It's about the taking."

Pancake rummaged in his cart and pulled out a loaf of bread. He handed it to Jeremiah, who rotated and judged it. Then he bit into it. He chewed and processed, judging the bread's quality, then shook his head, dropping the bread onto the pavement for his dogs.

Pancake sifted and searched in his cart, growing desperate. Then, although devastated to do so, he carefully slid a rectangular item wrapped in a towel from the rack beneath the cart. It was a DVD player. I hadn't seen one in a decade. Jeremiah was intrigued though. He examined it like a novel technology, something unknown to this planet. He pressed a single button as if it told him everything he needed to know about the device, then shook his head.

"What exactly is happening here?" I asked.

Pancake held up his hand, warning me to stay out of it.

"Can I give you some money?" I pulled out five dollars. "Will this help?"

Jeremiah pocketed my money. "Your money is no good here," he told me. Then he walked away, gesturing for us to follow him. Five minutes later we were back along the L.A. River, headed south toward Downtown and the port. I asked Pancake what we were doing, why we had to follow Jeremiah, but he kept telling me not to worry about it. He seemed worried himself though.

"Are we in danger?" I asked.

"No," said Pancake. "It's only how it is."

As we got closer to the city, the number of homeless dwellings along the river increased. No longer were there individual tents. There were full-blown communities: tents and huts and tarps tied together into mega-encampments, with each cluster having its own mound of trash, its own stockpile of stolen goods, and its own unique architectural style.

Some of the shelters were more like burrows. If you were a jogger just passing through, you wouldn't notice them. Not only because you'd be keeping your head down, hoping not to be shanked with a screwdriver, but because these caverns were amazingly discrete. They were mud huts, tunnels dug into the riverbank or into the hills alongside overpasses, with twigs and tarps and leaves and plywood reinforcing the walls.

There were a range of outdoor activities taking place among the natives. Half of the population were napping, a quarter were repairing stolen appliances or bicycles, and the last quarter were destroying things. There was also one woman facedown and motionless in the dirt, baking in the sun, with one shoe on. I was worried that she was dead. Maybe we should check on her, I suggested. But Jeremiah assured me that everything was okay. The woman was a friend of his, her name was Naomi, and they had already confirmed that she was dead. Arrangements were being made.

I liked the clear delineation of options around these parts. To me, this land provided possibilities no different than anywhere else: sleep, build, create chaos, or die.

One of the villages had a massive bonfire going. I watched as a man wearing only a leather vest, his penis right out in the open air, tossed a coffee maker atop the flames. There was something liberating about the scent of that burning plastic. This was a district of anarchy, a paradise. If the universe could fit into a box, these people would toss it onto the fire and start looking for the next thing to burn.

We approached the Taj Mahal of shanties. The ranch-style structure had a wooden skeleton, no different than a normal house, and it spanned a large area alongside the river. Countless extension cords connected it to a nearby overpass, tapping into the city's electrical grid. It even had a front door with a stained-glass window. I heard the muffled hum of generators as Jeremiah knocked three times.

"Say the words," said a voice behind the door.

"Bells and whistles," said Jeremiah.

The door opened, and in we went. We ducked through room after room of the labyrinth. People were shooting up on heroin, masturbating, playing checkers, clipping their toenails, reading books, smoking crack, breastfeeding, bawling their eyes out, and watching *The X Files*. Half of them seemed perfectly sane. The other half were lunatics.

We arrived outside what I assumed was the grand chamber, a ten-by-ten room with a peaked roof made from plywood and white plastic fences, the kind that normally enclose suburban backyards.

"Will your friend be joining?" asked Jeremiah.

"No," said Pancake. He gestured to a cinder block outside the door. "I'll be out shortly."

Jeremiah and Pancake disappeared into the room. I took a seat on the cinder block and waited. On the other side of the room, a nutcase woman was repairing an electric skillet. She waved at me and said, "Goodbye, Rebecca."

I waved goodbye.

She took the skillet and slithered out of the room, leaving me in silence. After a minute or so, I heard some clanging, then the smell of cooking meat filled the air. The nutcase popped her head back into the doorway.

"Rebecca," she said.

"I'm Rebecca?" I asked.

"I know," she said, smiling and nodding. "Everything will be alright for us now."

As she made her way toward me across the room, I realized that she likely thought I was her daughter. This role came with great pressure. How does one go about being a daughter? How could I make my mother proud? The task of womanhood seemed insurmountable. Women are pure and selfless and full of light. We men are tasked with nothing more than falsifying bravery and overeating. And I was yet to master either.

Mom grabbed me gently by the hand and guided me into the adjacent room, a long rectangular bedroom with a yellow tarp roof, in the center of which she was cooking an obscene amount of ground beef on her newly refurbished electric skillet. She'd loaded so much meat on there that half of it was spilling over onto the filthy oriental carpet. This overflow didn't bother Mother though, for she simply picked up the hunks of floor meat and piled them back on the stovetop, thus knocking more meat off, creating a kind of continuous meat waterfall. She was quite skilled at this, operating with full ambidexterity as she snatched up and replaced the meat scraps. This appeared to be her usual cooking method.

I sat down across from her and, in a mother-daughter moment, joined the cause, plucking gobs of meat off the floor and dropping them back onto the grill. There was a glow in mother's eyes as we worked in unison. She must have shared the fondest of memories with her sweet Rebecca. Perhaps the two of them had maintained this very meat waterfall when I was a young lady.

While Mom's culinary process seemed unhygienic at first, it became clear that she had everything sorted out on the sanitary front. She fetched an enormous glass bowl from underneath her bed and held up her hand, requesting that I pause the meat cycle. Then she swept all of the meat off the grill into the bowl. Next, she collected the floor meat and scattered it across the grill, killing off the microbes. Then she added that meat into the bowl and shut down the electric skillet. Meal complete.

Then people started filing in.

One by one, every member of the estate entered as Mother doled out plate after plate of ground beef. Everyone seemed to have an assigned seat around the room, filling out in a big circle. The last to enter were Pancake and Jeremiah, who seamlessly joined the pack. Once everyone had received a meat allotment, Mother made a plate for herself and took a seat beside me on the bed.

This was certainly a family. In fact, these people were the realest family I'd ever encountered. There were no secrets here. People masturbated and cried and smoked crack right out in the open. This ran contrary to the standard American family only in its public nature. Our nation's model families are rife with perversion and addiction and despair, but these great American pastimes are usually enjoyed alone in your bedroom or down in the basement, with the dining room being a kind of film set. Time for the dinner scene, folks. Here's the scenario: Dad cooked steaks. Splash some water on your face. Put on some makeup. Act sober. Smile. It's family time.

"This is Rebecca," Mom announced, placing her hand on my shoulder.

Most of the men in the room didn't even notice her introduction. They were too busy overeating, devouring their portions of meat. The women nodded and waved at me, welcoming Rebecca to the coalition. I couldn't discern whether they welcomed me because they were females, therefore warm by nature, or if they were also clinically insane and remembered me, the long-lost Rebecca. Pancake and Jeremiah were the only two siblings who gave me glances of suspicion. But they must have recognized the connection that Mother and I had forged, so they kept their lips sealed. It would have been a shame to spoil a perfectly good family supper.

Eventually everyone began exiting one after one into another room. I had no idea what the next family activity was. Perhaps it was dessert time. As the crowd cleared, Pancake caught my eye and, with a swift nod of the head, called for an exit. He disappeared, but I was too curious, so I took a peek into the next room over.

It was the stolen bike room. The whole crew began sorting and taking inventory on the day's plunder, with Mother delegating tasks. By my count, there were about twenty bikes piled high, a majority of which were children's bikes. One was so small that it had to be a toddler's cycle.

I'm all for theft, but this didn't sit well with me. Who steals from a child? Only children can steal from children. And adults can steal from adults. Or a child can steal from an adult. Those are the guidelines. It's the basic morality of theft.

I got lost trying to find my way out of the house until I realized I could just lift up the wall, made of an ornate tapestry, and exit. Pancake was smoking a cigarette outside, waiting for me on a stolen bike. He had another one for me. Both were adult-sized cruisers, fully eligible for heist.

"I assume they didn't give these to you," I said.

"That would be correct, my sweet little Rebecca-pie."

"What exactly just went on in there?"

"Everything costs something," said Pancake as he rolled away on his new bike.

UNCERTAINTY

If I was born in the 1400s, perhaps I'd have gotten my chaos fix by sailing the seas in search of undiscovered lands. Maybe I would have explored the western frontier in the 1800s. A century ago, I could have competed with the Wright Brothers in the aviation race. Today, though, what's a man to do? Tell me, where can one explore the fringes of the mundane? Am I supposed to traverse the planet and climb Mount Kilimanjaro? I'd never make it there. Because on every street corner in every city across the world there are sacred establishments, watering holes dancing with neon light, all of them shortcuts to beautiful pandemonium. Pour me some chaos, Gigi. I'll be here all day. Let's travel the world....

Chapter 9

Almighty God, I am sorry I am now an atheist, but have You read Nietzsche?
—John Fante

It was a bright and windy afternoon in what I believed was December. I wasn't sure though, so I decided to set a goal for myself: On the walk to Hugh Two, I would find out what day it was. The humans would be up to something that would divulge the date. They'd be going to church or taking a lunch break or hanging signs for Taco Tuesday. I could have just checked on my phone, but there's no honor in that. If you're going to lose track of the days, you have to find your way back onto the calendar the old-fashioned way.

It was certainly December.

There were Christmas lights everywhere. Herds of plastic reindeer. Gargantuan candy canes fastened to railings. Glowing trees in windows. Frosty the Snowmen. Ah, the holiday season. One day of the year when people can pretend to focus on giving, thus freeing up the other 364 days for selfishness, greed, and family neglect. It's all about balance.

It was Tuesday. I could tell because the east side of the street was mostly empty due to the parking regulations. The world was sending me signals.

"I can't believe this shit," fussed a man discovering a parking ticket on his car. He yanked it off his windshield. "The whole parking thing is a rip-off. The city's raking it in." He was talking to himself but hoping for a response from me.

I thought about chiming in, but I didn't know what to say. The parking rules are fairly simple. Once a week, for two hours, you can't park on a certain side of the street. I'm ardently against regulations, but on the scale of laws, this one is rather innocent.

"Don't pay it," I said in passing.

"And what'll that accomplish?" he asked.

"You get to keep the money."

"Yeah, and then they'll bang me with late fees and report me to the DMV," he snapped. "Then my car will be towed and impounded, I'll have no way to get to work, and I'll be out of a few grand instead of just paying a measly sixty dollars. Brilliant. Thanks for the input."

"Well don't give me all the credit."

"Excuse me?" he asked.

"I'm just saying, you deserve some recognition too. I mean, you're definitely an outlier at the very least. Despite the block being littered with clear and succinct parking signs that everyone else saw and comprehended, you left your car right here. That takes talent. You're a special man."

He did an angry movement with his arms but there were no accompanying words.

I casually continued: "And you claim to have a job, yet I just watched you walk out of your house in the middle of a Tuesday wearing pajamas. So, again, you deserve a pat on the back for somehow getting a company to pay you despite you not showing up. Although I'm not sure how you keep a job given the fact that you can't follow basic directions."

He stood there in silence.

I had no idea why I chose to eviscerate this man, but I was baffled that he had let me rant for as long as I did. It was quite a statement. It was all true though. I wasn't just saying my piece. I was dispensing reality. Maybe deep down he knew it was something he needed to hear. He craved the input of a harsh and objective third party.

"Who the hell works on Christmas Eve?" he asked.

That changed things, of course.

"Actually, I'm asking the wrong person." He turned back toward his house and, once safely on his porch, said, "What would a homeless person know about work?" He went inside and slammed the door emphatically, like he'd just won the confrontation.

I didn't even know it was Christmas Eve. I was as alone as one could be. A normal person would have been demoralized by this, but the gloominess of it warmed my soul. And the cherry on top was that this man thought I was homeless. I felt like this stranger had just handed me a trophy. I had been crushed and charmed by the black heart of fate.

The man's door swung back open. "Buddy..." he said.

I stared at him in admiration. I wanted to thank him.

"That wasn't right, what I said to you."

"Not a problem," I said.

"No, really, I shouldn't have said it."

I was losing respect for him by the sentence. Hoping to stop him, I said, "Seriously, it's not an issue. I actually—"

"It was messed up, and I'm sorry." He descended his porch. "Can I help you out? Is there something you need? Are you hungry?"

A few of his family members emerged on the porch behind him, waving to me like a zoo animal. They had probably scolded him for ridiculing me, a poor and damaged homeless man. And on Christmas Eve of all days.

His wife stepped up as the group's liaison, the head of catering: "We've got leftovers from lunch. Mashed potatoes and steak, green beans, whatever you want, sweetie. We can fix you a plate."

I was, in fact, very hungry, so I put on my most downtrodden face and nodded. They invited me inside, so I took a seat on the couch. The entire family, all nine of them, accepted me into the home with no hesitation, as if I was one of the siblings. A few of them carried on conversation, a few of them smiled at me casually. The grandfather even patted me on the back, a kind of *things will get better, young man.* In no way were any of them horrified about the potentially homeless man on their couch. Their ease with the situation really irritated me. I realized that this scenario would likely become some cozy story recounted for years to come: Remember when we fed that nice homeless man? I hope he's doing okay.

"How's your day going?" asked the grandfather.

The microwave beeped before I could respond.

Mr. Parking Ticket brought me over a heaping plate of warm food. He offered a plastic fork, but I disregarded it, barehanding a hunk of steak. I made outrageous faces, like a child tasting candy for the first time, as if I hadn't had a calorie in a month.

The meat was juicy and tender. It reminded me of the pot roast Poppy used to cook on holidays, but it wasn't quite as flavorful.

"I'm Rebecca," I said, chewing away.

This got everyone's attention. The family went fully silent.

I threw a large piece of broccoli into the fireplace.

"Now, now," said the grandfather, trying to calm me down.

"Who am I?" I asked him.

"You're Rebecca," he said seamlessly. He was handling the situation smoothly, going with the flow. "Come on now, take it easy, Rebecca. We're all friends here."

I moved on to the next family member, a woman in her thirties. "Who am I?"

Rebecca, she told me.

One by one, all nine of them assured me I was Rebecca.

Once I'd gotten them all to call me by my name, the room was totally silent for five or so minutes as I finished off my food in a totally docile state. I occasionally looked up and nodded at everyone, then went back to eating.

The wife eventually broke the silence. "Do you need anything else, honey?" She was hoping to get me out of the house. "How about some money for dinner? We'd love to help out with that. It's something we'd like to do." She shot a glance to her husband.

Mr. Parking Ticket pulled out his wallet and hesitated. He had plenty of cash—tens, twenties, even a few hundreds. His wife grabbed the wallet, trying to make things less awkward and facilitate the transaction. "How much would you like, sweetie?"

"$21.99," I said.

"Oh, well, okay, sure." She was taken aback by the specificity. "Here you go." She handed me a twenty and two singles.

"I don't have change," I said, scanning the room. "But if you give me a minute or two, I can find a penny. There's always one or two per square mile. That's what the science says."

"No, no, no, you keep it," said the wife.

"It's all yours," said the husband.

"It's a gift," said the wife.

"Merry Christmas," she said.

"Merry Christmas," he said.

The rest of the clan followed suit.

Merry Christmas, Merry Christmas, Merry Christmas.

"Wow, you guys are just dandy," I said. "Happy Jesus Day to you too. And thank you to everyone." What the fuck was I saying? I had no idea. I held up the cash to the light to ensure it wasn't counterfeit, then slipped it into my sock. They all nodded and smiled, hoping that was the end of the freak show. I could tell they wanted nothing more than to clean up the broccoli from the mantel and return to sanity. Thus, I continued: "Maybe they'll have some kind of holiday discount going on for the birth of our Lord, that way I can save a few bucks for later." I ran my hand across the sky as if two dollars could buy the galaxy. "But that's neither here nor there. If there's a sale, there's a sale. I don't set the prices. If I did, a bottle of rum would certainly be less than $21.99."

I laughed like a maniac and strolled out the front door. It wasn't so much an *I got you* cackle. It was wilder, more irrational, the stuff of a madman. I suddenly felt very uncomfortable. Walk, I told myself. Just get out of here.

It wasn't until I had made my way down the street, glancing into window after window at the many Christmas Eve gatherings, that I realized what had transpired: Those people had, for a few minutes, welcomed me into their family. Or at least tried. And it was something I so desperately needed. I was dying of loneliness. A solitude addiction, no different than a heroin habit. I was hooked on it, dependent, letting it kill me by the day.

That family did not see poverty. They saw loneliness. And they'd offered me treatment. But I had behaved like any addict would. I refused the help. I acted out of character. I went a little mad. I did what was necessary to get another fix. And it had worked like a charm: There I was, alone again on the sidewalk, getting high on isolation.

But it wasn't all doom and gloom. After all, it was Christmas Eve, and I had done what was right, much like Christ himself. I had sacrificed myself for a good cause. That family needed something other than each other's presence. Their gathering had been like most, boring and forgettable, a repeat of every other year. But I'd given them a story to tell, something to ridicule together. Remember that lunatic? What was her name? Rebecca.

They'd laugh at me for years to come.

I was a martyr.

* * *

Mr. John was sweeping the sidewalk.

He was so enthralled with the task that, not wanting to interrupt, I stopped to watch him before approaching. He would attempt to sweep a wad of chewing gum five or six times before realizing it was in fact a permanent part of the concrete mosaic. Then he would move on, skipping over shards of glass, used napkins, cigarette butts, and bottle caps en route to the next immovable clump of gum.

Perhaps he was well-aware that the gum was never going to budge. Maybe that was the point. He sought out the gum because it wasn't like the trash and the glass, which could be easily swept away in an instant. The gum was an unconquerable challenge. Each unyielding wad brought the prospect of hard work with no reward. It was about the struggle itself. Mr. John was either a kind of modern-day Sisyphus or he was useless, timelessly wise or grossly incompetent. Discerning between the two is often impossible.

"Merry Christmas," I said, giving him a little shoulder rub.

"Merry Christmas for you," said Mr. John. He set aside the broom and tried to rub my back while I was still rubbing his, but it didn't work logistically. So I deliberately stopped and turned my back toward him, accepting a back rub. He performed a vigorous, powerful massage. The physical labor must have kept him young.

"You have very tightness," he said. "Big knot, like a big rock."

"It's the stress," I said.

"The stress, yes." He dug his elbow into me. "You have the stress."

"More like depression," I chuckled.

"Yes, yes." He leaned close to my ear, massaging away. "You are on a depression."

There's a good book title in there somewhere, I thought. To be *on a depression*, as opposed to *in a depression*, makes sadness sound premium. The word *on* evokes a sense of superiority. Kings sit *on* thrones, God sits *on* high, we go *on* vacations, we get high *on* drugs. This thought soothed me. My earlier reflections had been correct: Loneliness is indeed a narcotic, a potent and delightful formula, and I had been hooked on it for years. A honeymoon with myself. My apologies, my friends, I'm unable to make it to your wedding. Or your birthday. Or your funeral. Or anything, really. I'm currently on a depression.

Mr. John requested a cigarette as payment for the massage. I gave him two, then rolled out my shoulders, testing my flexibility. The knot at the base of my neck felt entirely relieved. It was glorious. I was young and loose and ready to hunch over in a barstool for ten hours, thus allowing the knot to come back stronger.

"If you keep giving me massages, Mr. John, I might just snap out of it. It'll lift the darkness. I won't be on a depression anymore."

He shook his head.

"Are you saying no to the massages or no to the idea that they'd cure me?"

He resumed sweeping and said, "It does not depend on me."

I went inside.

Pancake was tossing popcorn into the air by the Christmas tree, yelling, "Wisconsin!"

"Do it again, Pancake!" Gigi pointed the soda gun at him. "Go ahead, have your fun in the snow! See what happens, motherfucker!"

Pancake did not hesitate to have his fun. He screamed something that sounded like his own rendition of the *pa-rum pum pum pum* from the Drummer Boy song, then launched a full tray of popcorn into the air, dropping a snowstorm on the entire bar. Everyone clapped as Gigi blasted him with soda from the soda gun.

An individual piece of popcorn landed on Penny's lap. She fed it to her baby nephew. The youngster had an early start on the local diet.

A sweaty Edgar popped his head out of the kitchen to see the action, but he was utterly unfazed. He bit into a chicken wing and nodded as though, before emerging, he'd speculated as to what was unfolding and the scene matched his prediction perfectly. He ducked back into his domain.

Gigi's punitive measures came to an end when Pancake dropped to his knees and started accepting the stream of soda into his mouth. In came Mr. John from the front. He started sweeping up the popcorn, hoping to push it under the Christmas tree, but it was getting soaked in soda. He surveyed Coke Lake and decided it was too daunting. "Bad man, bad man, bad man…" he said as he walked back to the front door.

I lit a cigarette and wished my brethren a Merry Christmas. It was a special night, a commemoration of Jesus. Thankfully you don't have to believe in God to celebrate his sweet baby boy. Families around the world would be feasting on turkey and cracking open their most expensive bottles of wine. We were no different. The popcorn machine was cranking. We would drink our usual drinks but just have more of them.

* * *

Penny handed me a scratch-off ticket at midnight. "Merry Christmas."

"No, no, you keep it," I said, passing it back to her. "I don't deserve it."

"Yes, you do." She set it down on the bar. "Merry Christmas, fucker."

"He really is a fucker," said Gigi.

"Big time fucker," Lana chimed in.

"The ultimate," said Penny.

"Thanks, ladies." I was loved.

Penny even brought a few extra scratchingtons and gifted them to two first-timers, complete strangers, sketchy train-hoppers from San Francisco. Once everyone had tickets, Penny lined up some Frankie Miller on the jukebox. Before pressing play, she made an announcement: "This is all so nice. We should say a Christmas greeting, like a prayer. Should we say a prayer? Does someone want to say something?"

"No," said Lana.

"No," said Gigi.

Everyone agreed: There would be no gratitude, no prayer. Who was there to thank? If there was a God, he'd be very confused by a prayer from us. Why are these heathens singing my praises? All they do is drink and sin and laugh at me. Are those scratch-off tickets, Peter? Am I seeing this correctly? My eyesight is starting to go. But are these people gambling mid-prayer?

"Scratch-a-latch!" shouted Pancake.

"*Pa-rum pum pum pum*," he bellowed, this time getting the lyrics correct.

On came "I'm Ready" by Frankie, and we scratched away. An asbestos mist began floating down from the ceiling. It was a white Christmas.

Every person's temperament shines through while scratching a scratch-off ticket. Mr. John was methodical and patient. Pancake was not. Gigi couldn't care less. Edgar was imagining retirement on the Mexican coast. One of the train-hoppers pulled out a straight razor from his front pocket and used it to shave his scratch-off.

As I watched it all unfolding, I couldn't help but feel a certain momentum building. Maybe there was a God, a benevolent consciousness about the universe, and it's during moments like these that it unveils its underlying will and purpose.

We all lost.

I made my way around, collecting the tickets and offering solace: "The odds of all these tickets being losers, not one winner at all, not even a single dollar or a free ticket, is actually something to be celebrated. I think the odds of us winning one was actually higher than the odds of us doing what we just did. This is a Christmas miracle, guys. We don't just lose. We lose big. And we lose together."

"Our own little family," said Penny.

"You're retarded," Gigi told me.

I thanked her.

I hung all the losing tickets on the Christmas tree, then returned to my assigned stool. Sitting there, I noticed something I'd never seen before: a series of small photos hung up behind the bar, partially obscured by a row of liquor bottles. There were ten photographs, each a headshot of someone sitting at this very bar. I leaned over for a closer look: seven men, three women. They seemed like a biker gang, weathered and hard, pickled by life, faces you'd see in an A.A. meeting or a prison.

I consulted Pancake and he didn't recognize any of them.

"They're from before your time," Gigi said.

"Is it a wall of fame sort of thing?" I asked.

"You could say that," she said.

"How does one go about getting his picture up there?" I asked.

"I wouldn't recommend it," said Gigi. "Half of them are dead."

"That can be arranged," I said.

"Yes, you're on the right track," she said, pouring me a shot.

Down it went.

Into the bathroom I go.

Drip, drip, drip.

The pulse of a world misled.

I'm simply an accident. Why take it all so seriously?

I can hear Edgar cheering through the wall. His team must have scored.

What a place this is.

How else would one go about a life?

* * *

"It's nice to sit," says Nanna.

"It is," I say.

"Well, you would know, wouldn't you?"

"I would," I admit, slapping the trusty dining room table.

She sighs, unamused. "We leave you unattended for a while and the next thing we know you're off eating someone else's pot roast and drinking the days away."

"I only ate the pot roast because they thought I was homeless. I was playing a character."

"We're all playing a character," she says. "It's about picking the right one."

"I've considered becoming a full-blown Caribbean pirate as well," I say.

"Har-har," she says. "You think it's doing you any good to sit here all day like this and—"

"He knows it's not doing him any good," Poppy interrupts, entering from the kitchen. He gifts Nanna a glass of red wine. "A gift from Dionysus."

"Nietzsche signed his letters as Dionysus," I say.

"Once he went insane, yes," says Poppy. "It's a cautionary tale, that one."

"Cautioning against what?" I ask.

"I'm not quite sure," says Poppy. "Arrogance, perhaps. Syphilis. Stupid mustaches."

"You had a stupid mustache for the whole of the 1960s," says Nanna.

"And it landed me with you," says Poppy. "Case in point."

Nanna playfully smacks his leg.

"I think Nietzsche realized his whole outlook was bullshit," I say.

"Go on," says Poppy.

"You're getting him too involved here," says Nanna, trying to nudge Poppy toward the kitchen. "This was supposed to be a strict wine delivery. The pot roast is going to burn."

"Well think about it," I say. "The guy who insists that God is dead ends up signing his own letters as if he's a god. What would drive him to do that?"

"Lunacy," says Poppy. "He thought some men were gods, himself included."

"The almighty Ubermensch," says Nanna mockingly.

"Yeah," I say. "But what does that accomplish? It doesn't get rid of gods at all. It just brings them down to the earth, right here in front of us. And that's a lot of pressure. So, our boy Nietzsche was sitting there trying to be a god amongst men, an Ubermensch, but as he got older and wiser, he realized that he wasn't even close. And I think we can all agree on that. We know about Nietzsche's life. He was mostly pathetic. But that's beside the point. It's not about the idea that Nietzsche wasn't an Ubermensch. It's that no one is. And that's what drove him mad. He realized that we're all pretty much equally worthless, and no one is any better than the rest. And the weight of that realization ruined him. So he tried to reverse course. He tried to resurrect the very gods that he killed. He started signing letters as if he's Dionysus or Jesus Christ. Those letters were his last attempts to bring the old gods back to life because he overestimated the human race."

"That's just plain awful," says Nanna.

"You've been thinking, at least," says Poppy. "I'll give you that."

"Oh, just tell it like it is," snaps Nanna. "He's got a drinking problem."

"I'm more worried about the thinking," says Poppy.

"I'll think you under the table," I say.

Poppy smirks. Nanna smacks his leg, this time with some venom. "What are you, a sadist?" she asks Poppy. "You want him to go through what you went through?"

"Of course not," says Poppy. "But me being the one who did go through it, that has to count for something. And I assure you, it's the thinking that's the root of his problem."

"Thinking and drinking go hand in hand," says Nanna.

"The chicken and the egg rears its ugly head again," I say.

"Philosophize all you want," says Nanna. "It won't get you anywhere."

"Yea, well, at least I'm alive, bitch."

A bluebird shrieked out in the yard.

There I was, alone in the dining room, a shaft of dawn reflecting off the table's rum-glazed surface. I smelled lasagna burning.

Another night had become another day.

<u>WOMEN</u>

If a wild animal or a blood-thirsty crack addict charged in here and attacked a woman, I would strike down the ravenous beast. I'd stab it in the jugular with a pool stick or smash a bottle over its head. The woman would then recognize me as a worthy mate, capable of protecting a family and wielding a sharpened pool cue. Pheromones would surge, and she would love me, at least for a few minutes. We'd go out to the Beauty to procreate and maintain our lineage. And the woman would stick around so I could help raise the child. Man protects woman, an ancient story, the lifeblood of evolution. The world was, for most of human history, an unthinkably vicious habitat. If you wanted to survive, you had to team up with someone. Woman needs man for protection, man needs woman because she is the key to humanity, the carrier of life. In this cruel modern world, though, we have lost our crucial starting point: imminent danger. This was a key ingredient of the bond between man and woman. Did ancient woman fall in love with ancient man *because* he saved her from the saber-toothed tiger or because he *eventually would?* The latter. Mates were found prior to threats, not upon their emergence. If you sense a barfight is developing, you do not wait until the first punch is thrown to warn your friends. Point being, with no built-in threats, there is no need for preemptive pairing. Without preemptive pairing, there is no clear avenue for man to fulfill his primeval purpose of protecting a mate. Such is my key point: Man is more adept at protecting a mate than finding one. Finding one was never an issue. It was about protecting her. As preposterous as it sounds, man is perhaps better suited to die for a woman than to ask for her telephone number. In today's world, women survive just fine on their own. They thrive independently. Man, therefore, often finds himself laughable and purposeless, lusting over black-haired maidens across the bar, knowing that if he were to approach, he would become the very threat he is evolutionarily designed to fight off. Can I buy you a drink? No, I have my own money, and I know you're only offering to buy me a drink because you want to procreate. That's only part of it, my dear. And you cannot blame me. A man has urges. I would die for you. Sir, you're creepy, and it's scaring me. Please go away or I'll call my boyfriend. Ah, okay, I understand. You already have a protective mate. This really came full circle. As you were....

Chapter 10

Laugh at the world's foolishness, you will regret it;
weep over it, you will regret that too.
—Søren Kierkegaard

I went grocery shopping this morning.

Most of this task is very straightforward. First, I check the rum prices. If they have a good deal running, I load some bottles into the cart. But this is rare. Their prices are usually no better than Port Liquor, and I like to support the mom and pops, so I move along to the frozen lasagna.

The rest of the process looks like this: I fill the entire cart, up to the brim, with frozen lasagnas. They're rectangular and small, thus easy to stack, so I do the job properly. I imagine myself as an Italian bricklayer from Abruzzo, a master of his craft. If diligent, one can fit forty-eight frozen lasagnas in the main cabin of a shopping cart, with an additional eight boxes on the upper deck. The undercarriage could house more boxes as well, but it's superfluous to even consider, for the store never has more than fifty or so lasagnas in stock, all of which end up in my cart.

The last step of my shopping involves finding one more item, something other than lasagna, to place in the cart. I do this to deter the cashiers from commenting things like: *Just lasagna?* or *Looks like someone's having a lasagna party.* In the case that the cashier does make a comment, thanks to my extra item, I can scathingly reply: No, moron, look closely, there's a bottle of soy sauce tucked in there among the bricks. That was my item of choice today: soy sauce.

When I got into line, I knew immediately that the cashier was going to make a comment. He was a chipper kid in his late teens, plagued with youth and idealism, who was yapping to every customer that passed through his lane.

I rolled my lasagna haul up to the register.

"It's the Great Wall of Lasagna," said the kid.

"Soy sauce," I told him.

"Yeah, a Chinese ingredient," he said. "The Great Wall of Lasagna..."

Suddenly I got the joke. I was taken aback by the young lad. This was a decent joke, a thoughtful quip that had gone right over my head. I scrambled, thinking, hoping a sharp response would come to mind. But nothing did. I just started unloading the lasagnas onto the grocery belt and said to him: "Forty-eight of them fit in the main cabin."

"Is that right?"

"Eight up top."

"Eight first-class seats, got it," he chuckled.

"And if you guys had more of them in stock, I could use the undercarriage. There's plenty more room down below." I remained deadly serious, business-like, gesturing to the rack below the cart.

"Sorry about that, sir," he said sincerely.

"There's no question that it would hold, structurally speaking," I continued. "So long as space has three dimensions, I can stack bricks. I've been at this a long time."

At this point, the kid was sufficiently creeped out. He kept his head down, scanning lasagna after lasagna. My goal had been achieved. Never again would this boy have anything clever to say about my lasagna habit.

* * *

Bumper and I had been playing pool for a while.

He's a terrible player with no respect for the game. He rambled as I tried to concentrate, rambled when he should have been concentrating, and showed zero appreciation for my impressive shots. It's no fun winning against someone who doesn't know what talent looks like.

I hit six balls straight to win.

"Good gracious," said Bumper, his eyes tracking someone near the entrance. I heard high heels clonking on the rotting floor. Turning, I spotted a tall, cripplingly good-looking woman in a swanky red dress, her hair as black as night. An expensive handbag swung from her shoulder.

If Pancake was here, she'd have been immediately accosted and labeled a Josephina, a female Joseph A. It wouldn't matter to Pancake if this debutante was in fact wealthy or, as was more common, pretending to be. Both were mortal sins in the eyes of Pancake. He somehow manages to look straight through beauty into someone's soul: pure objectivity, regardless of gender.

The woman approached the bar and had words with Gigi, handing her some type of pamphlet. Then out she went, gone like the rest of them, another stranger in high heels. Why do they never come my way and ask about my hopes and dreams?

"Who was that?" I asked Gigi.

"She's not as pretty up close," said Gigi.

"What did she want?" I replied.

Gigi tore up the pamphlet. "Just another parasite trying to peddle some bullshit." She tossed the scraps into the trash.

I spent the next ten minutes staring into my rum, making the ice cubes race around the track, playing out a scenario in my head: The black-haired beauty never left the bar. She asked to use the bathroom, so I ushered her back there. Right this way, darling. As we walked, I explained a few things to her: You and I, this could work. Sure, on the surface, we appear to be incompatible. You are classy, I am a disgrace. You drink champagne, I drink rum. You have money, I do not. But these distinctions are shallow, I hope you know that. Why do you chase money anyway? Money is the great destroyer. It clouds judgment, no different than love. But at least love comes with a lover. It's symbiotic by nature. What does money come with? Money is only a means to buy things. And to be bought is to be corrupted, compromised. That's why money ruins art. The minute money comes into the picture, art becomes something a little bit less than art. Hence the reason popular culture is a cesspool. It's where the money is. *The loveliest melody in the world becomes unbearably vulgar once the public start humming it.* Do you like Huysmans? Probably not. Anyway, it's best to exist outside of mass culture. I myself am too ambitious for money. Silence ensued. The black-haired vixen did not inquire about this too-ambitious-for-money business, and I knew that was the end of our relationship. A curious mind would want to delve deeper into the nuance of such a statement. This woman was not a thinker. She just wanted to use the bathroom and be on her way. But just as she swung open the door, she turned back and said: Too ambitious for money? That's interesting, actually. It goes against everything this world sings to us. Yes, yes, I tell her, now you are starting to see. Allow me to elaborate: Ideas have always been the supreme currency. The American dollar is merely a fad, a trend, the soup of the day. Many currencies came before it, and many will come after it. Ideas, though, they're inflation-proof. They are gold that can be carried with no hands. They're immune to the markets. They can survive the collapse of governments. They can survive the collapse of anything but humanity. And should humanity collapse, with evolution playing itself out again, the dawn of ideas will be the most important event in the timeline. So then, tell me, who is more ambitious: the man chasing a dollar or the man chasing a thought? You sound very pretentious, sir. Yes, I know. Of course it's pretentious. We all have a cosmos of pride in us, let's admit it. And there's only a select few people with whom the ego should fully unclothe itself. The best egos are borderline celibate. I would never say this to a stranger. I'm only saying it to you because I feel like there is a potential connection here that—

"You guys still trying to rescue Camilla?" interrupted Bumper from the claw machine.

"Always," I said, making my way over to the machine and paying my fifty cents of tribute. On came the machine's happy jingle. The claw rose up into position, swaying back and forth. I commandeered it directly over Camilla.

"You've got this, man," said Bumper.

I shook my head.

Down went the claw.

I failed.

"You were so close!" exclaimed Bumper. "Millimeters!" He began scheming up strategies as to how we could extract Camilla. He even asked if Gigi had a key to the machine, which of course she did, so that we could just reach in and pluck Camilla out of there. Clearly Bumper did not understand the game. Camilla was precious because she would never get out. Her impossibility was her sainthood. If she were to get out, she'd become one of us. She would be hung from the Christmas tree, adored for a week, then forgotten in the alley. So long as she remained trapped inside the machine, she was safe from the world.

"Joeeeeey-boyyyyyy!" screamed Pancake, plowing in the front door with his cart. He smashed into a barstool and knocked it over.

"Pancake, please!" shouted Gigi.

"Joey has showy-ed!" belted Pancake. "He's here! He's here! He's here!"

"Who's here?" asked Bumper.

"Eat dirt," said Pancake.

"He's out front?" I asked.

"Front and center, Sarge!" he roared. "Mobilize!"

"Are you sure it's—"

"Green Cadillac!" interrupted Pancake. "License plate HYPR756!" He smacked me on the ass and dragged me toward the front door.

"Will you guys cut the shit?" urged Gigi.

"Bad man, good boy, bad man," said Mr. John as we exited.

Pancake pointed left, to the nearest intersection. "He made a Lucifer right there."

"So, he's gone..." I said.

"The fucker was parked right here. He was staring into the door, checking the place out again, that fucking lifeguard! He's back to rescue us all!" Pancake kicked the wall, then punched a palm tree. "So I tap on his window, and I tell him that he's the one who's gunna need savin' because I'm gunna toss him with the sewer salmons!"

"I assume he didn't like that," I said.

"Nope! He took off south! But it took him thirty fucking seconds to drive from right here, right at this very spot, to that corner! I was damn-near keeping up with him myself! Together we can catch the fucker! Kaboomba!" He pitched the idea as if our speed would increase with each additional member of the team.

Mr. John stepped out the front door. "What is the trouble?"

"No trouble, Mr. John," I said. "Was there a guy out here though? A nice-looking guy? Green Cadillac."

"Yes, he was here," said Mr. John. "Do you have something to smoke for me?"

"We're in the middle of something here, Señor John," said Pancake.

Bumper joined us out front.

"Do you have your car here, fuckmill?" Pancake asked him.

"It's out back, yeah," said Bumper.

The last thing Pancake wanted was to include Bumper in anything, but we needed a car. He placed his hand on my back, leaning in close as if asking for forgiveness. "He and I, we are not comrades, capisce?"

I nodded.

* * *

Bumper braked as we raced toward a red light.

"No brakes," said Pancake from the back seat.

"I can't just—"

"Charge on through it!" screamed Pancake. "That's an order!"

Bumper followed the order.

"Left here," said Pancake.

"Can you explain to me what's going on?" pleaded Bumper.

"There's a guy we don't like," I explained. "And he just left Hugh Two."

"To go where?" asked Bumper.

"To his apartment," I said. "We think we know where he lives."

"Oh, we know," said Pancake.

"What'd the guy do?" asked Bumper.

"Everything," said Pancake. "Hang a Richard the Lionheart."

"Make a right," I clarified.

As we rounded the corner, I almost couldn't believe it. There he was, Joseph A himself, right outside the apartment building Pancake had claimed he lived in. He was dressed nicely, the light playing off his polished shoes as he hopped back into his green Cadillac.

We screeched to a stop behind him.

"Now what?" asked Bumper.

Pancake shook with fury. His teeth chattered. His arms flailed.

"Is he good?" Bumper asked.

I nodded.

Pancake swung open the door and hopped out. Just as his feet hit the pavement, though, Joseph A shifted his car into gear and pulled away. Pancake sprinted after him, but it was clear that he didn't stand a chance. Joseph A disappeared around the block, so we picked up Pancake on the nearest corner and continued the pursuit.

We followed Joseph A through the city, weaving through Downtown. He drove like a Joseph A: He did the speed limit, he made full stops, he yielded for pedestrians. Pancake kept insisting that we ram his car from behind, but I reminded him that we were drunk and in possession of narcotics. He would nod and caress the meth stash in his front pocket, then suggest the same tactic a few blocks later. Bumper tried to play some music, but upon seeing Bumper's phone, Pancake smacked it out of his hand. "Not on my watch," he said. Then he urinated in a beer bottle and tossed it out the window at a teenage bicyclist.

Eventually Joey-boy merged onto the 710 freeway. Bumper veered across two lanes to keep up with him and, given the daunting challenge of a major roadway, indulged in a few bumps of cocaine to keep focused. With lightning-fast hands, Pancake seized the baggie of cocaine from Bumper, frantically setting up generous lines for himself on the back seat. Bumper wailed in protest and swerved the car to a stop on the shoulder. He hopped out and rushed to the back door, but it was too late.

Pancake had made quick work of the bag. All the cocaine was now in his bloodstream. As Bumper attempted to salvage some of his precious powder off the back seats, Pancake calmly exited the car and took a dramatic, sensual breath of polluted air. "Joey-boy lives to see another day," he whispered.

Back to Hugh Two we went.

We parked right out front. When Bumper got out, Pancake climbed into the driver's seat and manually locked him out, demanding that he deliver us some drinks. Bumper unlocked the doors with his remote, but Pancake again locked the doors manually. They repeated this four or five times until Bumper threw his palms up, went inside, and returned with beverages.

We sat in the car and drank.

Pancake kept fiddling with the knobs on the dashboard, not because he was interested in their purpose but because he wanted to see which was the most pleasing mechanically. He would twist the A/C knob back and forth, mimic the noises with his mouth, then spend a moment deciding if he liked it. He ended up really fancying the clicks of the hazard lights button. He kept putting the lights on and off, on and off, mimicking the repetitive clicks. Eventually he didn't need the button. He just clicked himself.

"I've loved three women in my life," he said between clicks.

Bumper and I gave him our full attention.

He emphatically held up three fingers, a cigarette glowing in his hand. This lasted a very long time. He was frozen in this position for about a minute, perhaps painfully replaying one of his destroyed relationships. More likely, though, was that he just lost his train of thought. The cigarette burned his finger. He stomped it out on the carpet.

BLACKOUTS

I believe blackouts might be similar to dreams, in the Jungian sense. During a blackout, a drinker is campaigning for his future self. The mind is trying to sway itself, nudge the sober mind in the direction of self-realization. Thus, the version of yourself that comes out during a blackout is not a revelation of your true self. It is an artificial hyperbole, an archetype, a salesman, a fanatical politician tasked with making a point. If your blackout tendency is to get into fights, this isn't a sign that you should take up the martial arts. It's a sign that you should maybe toughen up in life's smaller battles. Stand up to your boss or your spouse. And if you're one of those drinkers who gets overly emotional and starts hugging everybody, or seeking out companionship, you shouldn't become a therapist. You should lighten up. Buy a dog. Go on a date. Love something while the sun is up. Keep in mind, this outlook of mine regarding blackouts is purely theoretical. More likely than not, it's nothing more than a means of rationalizing my own mistakes. It is never advisable to drink yourself into a state of non-recollection. It's simply a bad idea. And while this rule sounds very straightforward, I have always struggled with the logistics. I continue to pour my way into amnesia, waking up in horror, and telling myself things like this: On average, life is a thing we forget. Most events don't make the memory roster. Is it such a big deal, then, to not remember how I got here?....

Chapter 11

*The advantage of a bad memory is that one enjoys several times
the same good things for the first time.*
—Friedrich Nietzsche

The house was cold.

I tinkered with the thermostat for a few minutes but had no success. I wasn't too worried about it. Southern California only gets so cold. Upon trying to take a shower, though, I discovered that there was no hot water either. Every sink in the house ran ice-cold. I made my way into the kitchen and tested the stove: no gas.

I prepared myself some rum and called the city's gas department. I had six drinks before I managed to get someone on the line.

"What's the emergency?" asked the man. "Do you smell gas?"

"I don't have an emergency," I said. "I just pressed the emergency button because I knew it was the only way to get a living, breathing human on the phone."

"Sir, this line is for emergencies."

"Well clearly there aren't many emergencies happening right now," I retorted. "Otherwise you wouldn't have answered my call. You would have had me on hold for six drinks like every other operator."

A long silence told me I was correct.

"What's the issue, sir?"

"My gas got shut off."

The man asked for my name and address, then put me on hold for another drink. Upon returning, he told me: "You haven't paid your bill."

"So they just shut off my gas with no warning?"

"Usually they send a notice."

"There was no notice," I assured him. Truthfully, though, the mailbox was packed to the brim. I hadn't opened any mail in a year because it was mainly from the IRS. At one point, I asked the mailman to just place all my mail directly into the trash, but he said it was a federal crime.

"I can send someone out to get it turned back on," said the man.

"Please do."

"But when you get your next bill, make sure to update your payment method, because it looks like your last three payments failed."

"I can give you a different credit card."

"You can sort that out once you receive your next bill," he said. "The first step is getting someone out there to turn your gas back on."

"Okay, and when will that be?"

"The earliest time slot I have is next Tuesday at ten in the morning."

"Next Tuesday? I'm supposed to go a week without gas?"

"I'm sorry, sir," he said politely. "We're really busy right now."

"There's no way to speed this up?" I asked. "This is a joke."

"You could always walk over to city hall and see what they say."

"If I have to walk over to city hall, I'm bringing a firearm."

"Sir, please—"

"That's how these things start."

"Sir, I will call the police if I have to."

"No, no, don't call the cops," I said. "I'm joking. I don't even own a gun. It's just frustrating, that's all. I just want to take a goddamn shower."

"I understand, sir," he empathized. "You just have to give us a little time."

"A week is more than a little time," I said. "I know I said I don't own a gun, but, realistically, I could go out and purchase one, do a few days of logistical planning, and march my way over to city hall before I can manage to take a hot shower."

There was prolonged silence.

I was forced to break it: "I'm kidding about the gun, okay? I'm just making a point. It tells you something about our society, doesn't it? You want heat? Just be patient. It'll take a week. You want a gun? Here you go. Here's a fully automatic rifle. That's the trigger there, near the bottom, that little curved piece. In God we trust."

"Sir, these calls are recorded for quality assurance," said the man.

"Oh, there is no quality here," I said. "I can assure you that."

"You sound like a very unhappy person," said the man.

I hung up and paced about the living room.

All I wanted was a hot shower. This crisis made me realize that hot water had become one of my necessary creature comforts. Warm water on the skin, a direct input of happiness, no effort required. Why couldn't I take the stoic approach and embrace a cold shower? It would be painful, yes, but struggle is a wisdom factory. I felt lazy and domesticated, just another modern human who, if born at any prior point in history, would have been deemed weak at birth and abandoned in the tall grass or tossed off a cliff. Even if my elders had let me live out of sympathy and I somehow managed to make it into my early youth, nature would get the job done. A man who can't even live without hot water: laughable. The ancient world would have eaten me alive. I would die before the age of five. The grave would require minimal digging. Just a small, shallow hole for a frail young boy who couldn't hack the cold water.

Bluebirds, please, save me.

I am with you.

I am not with them.

In my desperation, a memory surfaced: Pancake had once raved about the public amenities at the beach. Was there hot water? The details escaped me, but I decided to find out. I packed a bag of supplies, a towel and soap and clothes and the rum, and strolled the three blocks to the beach.

There was an endless supply of hot water.

I was one of four people using the showers. Two of the others were homeless, one man and one woman, both stark nude. The last member of our tribe was a hippie living out of his car. He wore a bathing suit. I myself opted to go fully nude. The showers were enclosed by concrete walls on three sides, so there was a privacy about it, an intimacy, just the four of us.

I soaped up and listened to the ocean.

We are all brethren here at the public showers, I thought. Just four human beings indulging in the luxury that is hot water. Where have all the public baths gone? The ancient civilizations had baths all over the place. Common hygiene is a great equalizer. There is something about the nudity and filth that dissolves societal strata. Take a look around, people. Our outfits are all the same price once we take the clothes off. And we all get dirty. Look, there's the emperor over in the corner, soaping up his penis. That penis is below average too. That's a peasant's penis at best. And there's the queen over yonder. She's covered in rashes, an awful skin affliction. Her breasts sag down to her hips. Gravity doesn't take bribes. You see, we're all in this together, citizens. We're flawed and filthy and exposing ourselves.

I started to cry.

I had tried admirably to fend off the sadness with clever thoughts and hot water, but the levees broke. I replayed the man's words: *You sound like a very unhappy person.* Yes, thank you, sir, I am a very unhappy person. And now I am crying. But these are not so much tears of sadness. Me, this person in the shower, has grown immune to sadness. But there existed a former version of myself, now trapped somewhere deep in the cellar, who had a heart. He had a big heart. He felt things. He felt everything. That man would have been crying for a few years now. So these tears are for him. They are a remembrance, a yearning for that man. Come back, old friend. We need you. Everything is—

The naked homeless woman smiled at me.

She couldn't see the tears.

It was just hot water.

* * *

Some drifters had been playing pool for a few hours.

Through ten games, they'd taken very few difficult shots. A novice might have mistaken them for novices. But pool is a game of set-ups. If a player knows what he's doing, he leaves himself with only easy shots. To an idiot, aptitude looks like boring luck. But Pancake and I knew the difference.

These gentlemen, while certainly in need of a trip to the public baths, were pool aficionados. Such is the beauty of pool. It does not discriminate. Woman or man, rich or poor, black or white, hillbilly or royalty, it doesn't matter. A fat, drunk, low-I.Q. degenerate can dominate a world-class athlete. One has either logged his time on a pool table or he has not.

"You liquid?" asked Pancake.

"Possibly," I said. "What are you thinking?"

"Come in low," he said. "Ten bucks."

"Creep up like a jaguar," he whispered to himself.

"Then we crank her up as the soup simmers," he said, stirring an invisible cauldron.

I said I was in.

"You fellers fancy a game?" Pancake asked the men.

The drifters exchanged looks, then nodded. They were in.

I noticed their scuffed backpacks tucked under the pool table. Drifters like this came in every now and again. They're the truly homeless types. They grow no roots. They have no favorite bar, no specific sleeping spot, no routine, no home city. They run from their past day after day, an endless pursuit. I respect the lifestyle: I'd run too if I had the work ethic.

It was agreed upon that we'd start with ten dollars per game. Pancake instructed Penny to play strictly Frankie Miller, threatening her with strangulation if another artist came on.

I smacked the opening break as the plaster mist began floating down from the ceiling, and what occurred next was nothing short of magic. I ran five straight racks, not missing a shot. We took them for $10 twice, then $20 three times, all without anyone but me shooting a single shot. I even took stripes two of the games, inherently giving us one extra ball because of the missing seven, but that couldn't slow my roll. I was unstoppable, in a drunken zone state. Time did not exist. I was a thoughtless wonder. I lapped the table hitting ball after ball, a walking miracle navigating the asbestos haze. After each ball went in, Pancake did jumping jacks, berated the poor drifters, and tossed me the chalk.

The only lull in the action came when a fly landed on the eleven ball. We were forced to pause the game for ten minutes. The drifters kept saying that we should shoo the fly off, but Pancake called them fuckmills and flashed his switchblade. He told them that if anyone was going to get shooed away, it was them.

So we waited.

The drifters ended up only having $23 dollars on them, so we shook hands and they promised to pay us back eventually. I knew I'd never see them again.

"I have a bet," said one of the drifters. "We play one more game, and I'll bet you all the money we've lost thus far that you don't run out again."

I chuckled. Of course not. We were up big.

"Done!" screamed Pancake, returning from a meth session in the alley.

No balls went in off the break.

With a single shot, we lost back all the money we'd won. Then we lost four games straight and went down $40 because Pancake was in full meth stroke mode. He yelled *kaboomba* after every shot then strummed away on his pool cue guitar, single-handedly ensuring our defeat.

But it didn't matter. A miracle had happened here. It was unanimously agreed upon that my five-rack run was the stuff of folklore. I'd become a world-class athlete, one of those people who picks a craft, masters it, then performs it with perfection over an extended period of time. It was the greatest twenty minutes of my life. All of my hard work had paid off. I had logged my hours, spilled my blood and my sweat and my drinks, and everything had come full circle back to this very table with its three-degree tilt and its faded felt and its missing seven ball.

We joked about that missing seven ball. We said it probably ran off one night because it was tired of this fucking place, tired of the drinking, tired of all of us, tired of its life being confined to a faded three-by-seven table in a place with no dreams. Perhaps it was only me, in my own head, who was joking about that seven ball. But it was a good thought either way. Sometimes it's hard to remember which ideas make it out into the wild.

Nonetheless, I was a champion.

I didn't pay for a drink all night.

I assume there were many.

* * *

She climbs on top of me.

She softly bites my neck, then spins around, doing a one-eighty. She somehow maneuvers herself gracefully in the confined space, her leg swinging by my face, her ass settling front and center before me.

"You know us big girls," says Gigi. "We know where things go."

Good lord, I've always known her ass is huge, but this thing is a force. It's too big for me, I think. Yes, yes, far too big. I'm just a boy trapped in this adult vessel. Gigi needs a man, a real man, a lumberjack or a steamfitter, someone who knows how to operate a forklift.

The name *Frank* is etched into the Beauty's metal roof. It looks like it was carved with a jagged rock. A petroglyph, a vagrant cave drawing. I love archaeology. I really do. It's fascinating.

I chuckled to myself and played it cool.

Daytime, it was certainly daytime. Clouds were scattered across the sky, so I gathered that it was early, the sun yet to burn away the morning gloom. Everything snapped into focus, became itself: the dumpster, the alley's brick walls, Pancake's cart stuffed to the brim with empty bottles and stolen goods, Gigi's caramel brown hair, the smooth skin on her back, the shards of broken glass, millions of them, shimmering on the fractured asphalt.

A garbage truck pulled into the alley, slowly passing us. The sanitation workers laughed and waved to us. We waved back. I wanted to ask if they minded tossing me away with the rest of the trash. Would you be so kind and chuck me in the back? Crush me with the hydraulic press, boys, just for the fun of it. I won't press charges. Gigi can keep a secret.

"Sorry," I said.

"Goddamnit," said Gigi. She shimmied off me, sliding out the trunk, nudging Pancake's cart out of her path.

"Not my best performance," I said.

"That's okay," she said.

"Yeah, sorry, I..." I wanted to provide solace, to tell her that it wasn't about her, that it was about me, about my thinking. The return of my rational mind had been the cause of the issue. If I'd just stayed in a state of incoherence, I probably would have been a stallion. But consciousness had ruined me, turned me impotent. I'd become sick with reason.

"Don't worry about it, honey," said Gigi.

I hopped out the side door and grabbed my rum off the roof. Gigi's casual nature terrified me. She was cool as can be, whistling as if she was in her own bedroom.

"Is this something you do?" I asked.

"Is what something I do?" she responded, buttoning up her jeans.

I gestured to the Beauty, then to myself, then to her: "This."

She squinted into my eyes, waiting for me to clarify something. I began to worry that I'd committed some unspeakable act. Did I force myself on her? Am I a monster? I nervously swirled the ice around in my glass.

"Are you kidding?" she asked.

I shook my head.

"Yes, this is something I do." She fixed her hair in the sideview mirror, then leaned within three inches of my face. "It's something *we* do."

I fidgeted, calibrating. "Wait, like...?"

"Yes," she said, disappearing back into Hugh Two.

I trailed her in. The bar was empty except for Pancake shooting some pool. As I passed, he muttered, "That was a fast one, buster."

I sat at the bar and locked eyes with Mr. John, smoking a cigarette in the entryway. He peered at me through his cloud of smoke. It was a sad, sympathetic stare. *You've been a bad boy, but these things happen.*

Edgar poked his head out of the kitchen, deviously raised his eyebrows at me and did a quick humping motion, then got back to work.

Everyone but me seemed to know about my encounters with Gigi.

"Drink this," said Gigi, setting down a water.

I tried to think back and remember something from our past, a sliver of a moment with her in the Beauty, anything. But there was only blackness.

"How many times?" I asked.

"Enough," she said.

"I thought you hated me," I said.

"Apparently not," she said.

"Well, that's some good news, at least."

"I'd call it a strong dislike," she said.

"There she is," I said.

"I don't want to get all emotional here," she said. "But it's not normal to not remember stuff like that. Even for this place, that's not good."

"Yea," I said. "Sorry."

"Don't you worry about me. Gigi's just fine. It's not me I'm worried about. You've got to slow it down with the rum."

A hazy sorrow drifted in. The mildew stains up in the corners, the cracking of pool balls, the aroma of frying wings, the hum of the popcorn machine, the rickety stool beneath me: They all became emblems of disappointment. Why must life shake us down so often?

I went out front for a smoke.

"Today," said Mr. John. "It's one of the cloudy days."

I nodded, looking up at the drifting clouds.

"A nice lazy day for the sun," he said.

If anyone else had spoken these words, it would have been small talk. But Mr. John was not a man for small talk. There was nothing small about the clouds and the wind and the sun. Maybe that was his message: *Look up, good boy. The sky is big. Your problems are small.*

My insignificance was soothing.

"Rain tomorrow," he said.

Now I couldn't tell if he was playing sorcerer and predicting my demise or merely regurgitating the weather forecast. I tracked the wrinkles on his face, the deep lines that enclosed his smile. Some of us look wiser as we age, as if life has left us with something. Others seem only more hurt.

I feared I was transitioning into the latter group, slowly losing pieces of myself, the pain telling a story on my face. I stood there, staring into the sky, and tried to imagine myself as an old man. But I drew a blank.

Will there be any of me left by then?

RELAXATION

For the intelligent mammal, relaxation is the act of worrying about things in a stationary position. To truly focus on your internal torments, it's best to be externally still. Hence the invention of the chair and the bench and the couch, with the bed being a kind of throne of anxiety, the finest place to lose sleep....

Chapter 12

We can regard our life as a uselessly disturbing episode
in the blissful repose of nothingness.
—Arthur Schopenhauer

Mrs. Connolly was dead.

Me and the rest of the bluebirds had really been letting loose recently, but there were no complaints, no knock on the door, no shouting from her window, no visit from the boys in blue. So every morning became a sort of beckoning to Mrs. Connolly. I squawked and squawked, but she never showed face. There was no sign of her. After almost a week straight at the dining room table, I settled on the hard truth: The old woman had perished.

I played out a few scenarios in my mind. The first one involved me running over to her house, slipping through a window, and administering CPR to save her life. This option quickly faded when, glancing around the room, I couldn't locate my pants. I usually wear the same pants for a week or two at a time, so this was strange. Finding them was going to require standing up and moving around and exerting effort. This, combined with the fact that I did not know how to perform CPR, forced me to move on.

The second scenario was worse. What if my thunderous squawking had caused Mrs. Connolly's death? She may have had a heart attack from the auditory shock. I saw the headline: *LOCAL WOMAN KILLED BY BLUEBIRD.*

At first, I felt a great pain for Mrs. Connolly. What had I done? But within minutes, I spun it in my favor. Her demise was nothing out of the ordinary. She was old, creeping toward death, and something was going to get her eventually. It just happened to be the sunrise squawking of a bluebird that put her in the dirt. At least she died of natural causes.

She also could have gone on her annual trip to Arizona to see her sister, the most plausible scenario, but that was no fun. I was in the mood for mortality. Nothing short of death would do.

I eventually sorted out the correct scenario in my mind. Here's what would really happen: One morning in the near future, Mrs. Connolly, returning from her vacation, would call the police. What's the emergency? She will inform them that, for the first time in a very long time, there has been no squawking at sunrise. Surely my neighbor, the bluebird, has passed away. Your neighbor is a bird? Yes, he's a bluebird. Go into his house and you will understand. The police send a car over. The officer walks into the dining room and finds me slumped over the table. I don't know what my exact cause of death will be, but they can just pick out of a hat: despair, alcohol poisoning, sleep deprivation, suicide, laughter, lunacy, etc.

An hour later the coroner arrives to examine my body. She is a tall woman with green eyes and a sharp intellect. Immediately, she feels a sense of importance in the air. This dining room is a hallowed chamber, this table an altar. Is this the corpse of the holy one, the bluebird himself?

In the center of the table, she sees a handwritten note that I have left for the world: *We are all dying. I was just very good at it.*

She finds this very profound, because it is, and she reaches for the note. But as she grabs the piece of paper, it sticks to the table. Maybe there is a pool of dried blood beneath the note, she thinks, causing it to stick to the table? She leans down to examine the table, running her hand along its surface. She smells her fingers. It's rum. The whole room, she comes to realize, is soaked in a fine veneer of rum. My God, this man is the bluebird, the one I have heard about. She again reads my note, observing my slouched and sacred body, and nods in agreement. The bluebird was right: We are all dying. And he was indeed very, very good at it.

* * *

"Mr. John," I said.

"The good boy," said Mr. John. "You stay at home for a few days."

I nodded. "A domestic bender."

"Do you have something to smoke for me?" he asked.

We smoked in the front doorway for a few minutes. Neither of us said a word until a fly landed on Mr. John's cigarette. "He will go," said Mr. John, continuing to puff. As the ember neared the fly, it took off just as Mr. John had said, buzzing into the sanctuary that is Hugh Two.

I did the same, stopping at the jukebox. I blew $10 to ensure that Frankie Miller's *Once in a Blue Moon* album played the whole way through.

"It's gunna be a good day, huh?" asked Penny.

"Probably not," I said. "But Frankie'll help either way."

"That he will," said Penny.

She tilted her head back and exhaled a plume of smoke away from the baby, toward the ceiling. You had to respect her concern for the child, making sure he experienced only minimal exposure to second-hand fumes. A little adversity is good for the immune system, but you don't want to overdo it. As Frankie's opening track came on, the baby began to cry.

"You're a lost cause," I told him. "Penny, Bud or tequila?"

"You're in some mood, huh?"

"Not particularly."

"One of each," she said. Penny only drinks Budweiser or tequila in a sequence of two to one. Two Buds, then a shot, repeat. She even carries around her own saltshaker and a plastic baggie of sliced up limes. If you ask her why she only drinks in this specific order, she responds the same way every time: *It's something my mother taught me.*

Gigi delivered Penny her drinks, then got around to mine.

"You had me worried," she said.

"I went to Hawaii."

"Really?"

"No."

"I thought you might have killed yourself," she said.

"I considered it."

"Too much work?"

"I'm just not done thinking about it."

"That's the spirit."

We ended up playing Shoe Clue once Lana had shot up and passed out in the Beauty. She woke up and came tromping in the back door, but Pancake and I forgot where we hid the shoe. He claimed I had hidden it. I claimed he did. A booze delivery driver named Marty happened to be there at the time and joined in on the search party. Eventually he asked an absurd question: Why had we hidden the shoe in the first place?

We told him to leave.

After searching the bar high and dry, there was no sign of the shoe. Lana kept smacking us on the head because she thought we were deceiving her. Really we'd fooled ourselves.

* * *

On the way home, I stopped at Port Liquor to restock on rum. Amir peered out the front door as I perused the candy aisle.

"Where is he?" asked Amir.

"He's not here," I said.

"Yesterday he throws a pepper at me," said Amir. "A whole vegetable, a perfectly good vegetable. He throws it at me and it hits right here on my chest, on top of my heart."

I met Amir at the counter with some rum and a chocolate bar.

"Rum," said Amir. "Rum, rum, rum."

"What color?" I asked.

"What color is what?"

"The pepper that he threw at you," I said. "Was it a bell pepper?"

"Why do you care about such a thing?"

"I don't," I said. "It was just a set-up to state the fact that it doesn't matter because all bell peppers are really the same from a genetic perspective. The variation in color is just determined by when they're harvested." I thought for a moment. "Actually that might be a myth. Is that an old wives' tale?"

"You think you are so very smart," said Amir. "And yet you walk around with the bad people." He reached beneath the counter and handed me a yellow bell pepper.

"Walking with the bad people," I said. "That would be a good book title."

Reaching into my pocket, I realized I had left my wallet at the bar. Amir begrudgingly agreed to loan me the rum and candy for a small interest fee.

"I'll be back soon enough," I said.

"Yes, yes, I know."

"Unless you want me not to return."

"No, no, you must return."

"Just say it for me," I said.

"If you do not break the rules, I do not say it."

I knocked a few bags of chips off the shelf to elicit the proper response.

"Do not return," said Amir.

I picked up the chips and placed them neatly back on the shelf. Then I bit the bell pepper like an apple and strolled out into the cloudless night. There I was in my own skin, perfectly coherent, having a decent go at it. The day had been the most normal one in a long time. I had gone to the bar, I had enjoyed time with friends, and I had closed out my tab before midnight. I remembered most of the day. The most wicked thing I'd done was steal Lana's shoe, but it would turn up eventually.

It always does.

POOL

Pool tables are a place of mathematical order. There is a method to the madness, Pythagorean in nature. One can always count on the pool table, even a beaten up 1978 Valley, to bring an Apollonian balance to the Dionysian chaos that rules every other inch of the bar. Pool tables are not like us. They are honest and steadfast. No matter the time, no matter how many drinks have been had, no matter how badly we don't want to hear it, the table tells the truth....

Chapter 13

Talk nonsense, but talk your own nonsense, and I will kiss you for it.
—Fyodor Dostoevsky

It was raining.

I quickly hopped out of bed and shut the windows, but it was too late. The floors were drenched. I tossed a few towels onto the affected areas and returned to bed. What time was it? I had no idea. What mattered, though, was that the sun had called in sick. The star of the show was taking a vacation day. In Southern California, such is always grounds for us to do the same. When the boss is away, the rest will play. I cocooned myself in the blankets. This was a day to relax, a holiday, a moment to unwind.

Granted, I didn't have a job, so a holiday might sound strange. But vacations are not about escaping a job. They're about escaping misery. And misery is not exclusive to members of the workforce. I know plenty of people, all of them perennially unemployed, who are in dire need of a vacation. Employed or not, each of us develops a routine to avoid being strangled by life, but in time that routine ends up wrapping its hands around our throat. The medicine becomes the poison. Everything loses its luster, including ourselves. And that's the real key: It's about us. We grow tired of what we become, because we stop becoming. We can blame the routine, whether the office or the bar, but it's really about the sneaky feeling that we've reached an undesirable homeostasis.

Wake up. Drink coffee. Work.

Marry. Multiply. Die.

Should a life be so easy to summarize?

I felt myself settling into a routine, the misery sharpening its blade. I had certainly developed predictable rhythms. More likely than not, I would exit my bed, I would sit at the dining room table, I would drink some rum, and I would become a bluebird.

But who among us can claim to be a bluebird?

Only one.

I have that going for me.

What do bluebirds do in the rain?

I exited my bed, I sat at the dining room table, I drank some rum, and I became a bluebird. Sitting there and singing, I listened for my fellow birds. But all I heard was rain, the clouds playing drums on the roof. So be it, I thought. If the rest of the bluebirds were going to take the day off, I would have to pull my weight. I would go it alone. The heavy rainfall provided cover, a guarantee that no one, not even the ghost of Mrs. Connolly, would hear me. So I belted away, testing my range and volume. A singular bluebird, the strongest of the flock, refusing to be stopped by the storm.

I sang and I sang and I sang.

Eventually my voice gave out.

That was enough for the day.

* * *

A random woman, so intoxicated that she could barely keep her eyes open, was slouched over the bar, ranting to Gigi. She claimed her uncle was a prince in the Middle East. I asked for more details, specifically what country her uncle ruled, but eventually she stopped speaking English. It wasn't that she shifted into a foreign language. It was that she started rambling in the most local language there was, that of an incoherent drunk, her words unintelligible, her saliva spraying her surroundings.

"She's a gypsy," claimed Pancake.

"Where are gypsies from exactly?" I asked.

"Nowhere," said Pancake.

"She lives in San Diego," Gigi clarified.

"I went to San Diego once," Penny chimed in. "I used to travel."

"I walked there once," said Pancake. "San Diego is a rat hole."

"How long did that take you?" I asked.

"Thousands of miles," he said. "Many, many thousands."

The gypsy woman eventually passed out on the floor. Gigi asked us to transport her out to the Beauty, so we did. I grabbed her legs, Pancake lifted her awkwardly by the head.

"Grab her under the shoulders," I suggested.

"No," said Pancake.

We only made it a few feet before Pancake dropped her head onto the ground. It slammed against the floor. "Carpets," Pancake said to me, as though that fully cushioned the blow. This time he picked up the gypsy by her ears, dropping her again a few feet later. Eventually we did make it out to the Beauty, but Lana was in there shooting up. So we hauled the gypsy back inside, planning to slide the body under the pool table. But there were piles of garbage and popcorn and broken glass under there. Gigi told Mr. John that the trash was a problem. It had to be cleaned up. Mr. John agreed. "Yes, yes, it is a big problem," he said. But he proceeded to not take any action whatsoever. He'd been eating an apple for two hours. He continued to do so.

"Put her in the women's room," said Gigi.

I felt like we were delivery boys being instructed where to put a couch. We again lugged the gypsy toward the back of the bar, arriving at the closed door of the women's room. I often forget that Hugh Two even has a women's room. Gigi has a very strict rule that men are never permitted in there. It's such a serious directive that even Pancake obeys it.

Pancake swung open the door.

We dragged the corpse in and plopped her down on the floor, one last concussion. Then we stood in awe of the women's room. It was spotless. No graffiti, no filth. The toilet and sink and tiles glistened a blinding white. The mirror had no cracks or blemishes. The scent of a strawberry candle brought a smile to my mind. There was even a nice framed photograph of sunflowers on the wall. Big, tall sunflowers, a field of them.

Pancake started to breathe heavily. Agitated, he scratched his scalp, shifting his weight back and forth. I could read his mind, because I felt it too. He wanted to put an end to this room. He wanted to destroy something, to make the pretty unpretty. Smash the mirror, piss on the floor. He wanted to treat these perfect things like he would treat a person convinced of his own perfection. This room was like Joseph A. It must be torn down. It must be told the truth.

"We better go," I said.

Pancake knelt down and yelled into the gypsy's ear: "So much potential!"

* * *

Those droplets are holding the universe together.

One evening I seated Beauty on my knees.

Drip, drip, drip.

And I found her bitter.

Down goes one into the abyss, out comes another.

And I cursed her.

"Everything okay in there?" she asks.

No, everything is not okay, Gigi.

"Are we playing or are we vandalizing?" she shouted.

"Playing," I responded. A game was being played, apparently. I slithered out of the bathroom and glanced around. The bar was empty. And it was dead silent, not even the jukebox was talking.

"Looking for someone?" asked Gigi.

"Just admiring," I said.

Gigi was standing alone at the pool table, a cue in her hand. I grabbed my stick and approached the table. Was I solids or stripes? My gut told me that I had courteously taken stripes, that I had given Gigi the one-ball advantage that comes with being solids. I hope you're out there somewhere, seven ball. I hope you've found love and peace and everything else that's missing. I shot the twelve ball into the side pocket, a brilliant slow-roller, setting myself up for the nine ball in the corner.

"Nice shot," said Gigi.

I knew I was a gentleman, that I had blessed the lady with the inherent advantage of solids. Nonetheless, my kindness had limits: I wasn't about to let her win. I made easy work of the nine ball, using heavy backspin to set myself up for the fourteen in the popcorn machine pocket. The cue ball stopped right on the money. This was all too easy for me. Down the fourteen went into the table's viscera, with the cue ball stopping dead in its tracks. There I was, perfectly set up for the eight ball. The game was mine.

"No mercy," said Gigi.

"Not usually, no," I said, lining up the eight ball. But as I leaned down to put Gigi out of her misery, I remembered the gypsy woman. "Is that lady still passed out in there?"

"No."

"She woke up, huh?" I said. "I thought we might've killed her."

"You walked her to her car."

I nodded. This must have been the case. There was no reason to question it. I had escorted the gypsy corpse to her car, another mark of a gentleman. "That women's room is quite the place," I said, directing the conversation away from my amnesia.

"Yeah," said Gigi. "It's crazy what can be accomplished if you actually clean something."

"It's a disquieting metaphor for the world at large," I said, bending down to shoot.

"Meaning?" asked Gigi.

I put my shot on hold and elaborated: "If we let women run things, that bathroom is what the world would be like. Things would be clean and inviting and there would be nice candles burning in the living room. But unfortunately, evolution fucked us, I'm afraid. Men got the egos, we got the muscles. This is a man's world. And our gender is selfish. We kick the doors down, we clog the toilets, we write on the walls. We seem to have no concern for anyone but ourselves. The next generation, they might as well not exist. And what's funny is, we ruin it for ourselves in the process. I mean, look at the men's room. It looks like a place we're actively trying to ruin. You women, you like to burn candles. We men like to burn the world to the ground."

I refocused and sank the eight ball. "Like I said, a man's world, Gigi."

"You're retarded," said Gigi.

"I know," I said.

"You're really not though."

"Not fully."

"You're too smart to be broke."

"Did I not pay my tab?"

"Your card got declined." She tossed my credit card onto the pool table.

"Fuck, sorry," I muttered, fumbling for my wallet.

"None of your credit cards work," she said.

My eyes met hers. Pure sincerity, that's what I saw. In Gigi's gaze was reality, the music I had been refusing to face. If the world had broken the news to me, it would have stung too much. So there was Gigi, messenger on behalf of fate: "You're fucking broke. You don't have a single dollar, your bank account is empty, the credit cards are maxed out. You could sell your car, but that would only float you for a few months. The only real options are to sell your house or go back to work. We established all this last night."

I combed my mind. The memory of such a conversation was not there, no images or words. But the emotion, the weight of it was there. It had trickled into my psyche. It reminded me of the smell after a heavy rain: I missed the storm, but I knew it happened.

"I knew this was coming," I said.

"I know," she said. "You told me that too."

"What else did I say?"

"Let's see," she said. "That you love me, that you're so sorry, that you'd pay me back as soon as you can, that you wouldn't be here today..."

"Sorry," I said.

"It's okay," she said. "But you really do have to figure yourself out one of these days or you're gunna end up like the rest of 'em. You'll be passed out in the women's room."

"I could always move into the Beauty."

"Good idea," she agreed. "Live off popcorn for a while, tide yourself over until you end up dead or in prison."

We laughed.

"You were solids by the way," said Gigi.

"Seriously?"

"You hit in four of my balls."

"Christ," I said. "Those were good shots though."

"Very good," said Gigi. "That's what happens when all you do is drink and play pool. Hitting balls isn't a problem. Hitting *your* balls is."

"I like that," I said.

Gigi smiled. I wanted to smile back, but I'm not sure if I did. She walked around the pool table and hugged me. I hugged her back, the glow of blue neon finding her hair.

"I'll figure it out," I said.

"I know you will," she said with a smile. "You have to. You owe me money." She roamed back behind the bar and began pouring a beer. "I'm switching you over to beer. All that rum isn't good for you. You're going to die before you get to write your book."

"Live fast, die middle-aged," I said.

I took my assigned seat and quickly did away with the beer.

A barstool is a throne outside of things, a place where dreams and memories and meaning don't get served. Over by the pool table, I owed Gigi money. I was a scoundrel, a Mitya, my life on the brink of collapse. But now I was again a king. And to sit atop this throne, your highness needs no birthright, no royal guard, no people to rule. There are no subjects here. Kingship requires only a drink. Gigi handed me another golden chalice. I did what I do to drinks. It became me. It is time to make a toast, a salute. Great men do such things. Up went my glass, bringing my arm with it: The great Gigi, mother of the medicine. You are it. You are the elementary truth. You are the keeper of this horrible place. Oh, my dearest Gigi, you are the closest thing to God. Do you know that? And me, I am no common man myself. I am royalty. I am King of The Ruthless Now.

"You're starting to scare me," says Gigi.

"Did I say something?"

"Please don't be here tomorrow," she says.

Fuck tomorrow, I tell her.

What did tomorrow ever do for me?

* * *

Students flood the streets. Poppy maneuvers the car through an army of children wearing uniforms: blazers and ties, button-down shirts and shiny shoes, dress pants and hair gel. All of them lug fifty-pound backpacks up the steep stairs toward the entrance.

"What do they have in their backpacks?" asks Nanna.

"Books," I say.

"Books are good," says Poppy. "But there's a fine line between literature and scoliosis."

"Where's your backpack?" asks Nanna.

"In my locker," I say.

"Didn't they assign you homework?" asks Nanna.

"I did it," I say.

"Without your books?" she asks.

"We've got all the books worth reading at home anyhow," says Poppy.

"I did it yesterday," I explain. "During school."

"How did you pay attention if you did the homework during school?" she asks.

"It's called multitasking," says Poppy. "It's either that or scoliosis."

"Will you cut it out?" snaps Nanna.

"I paid attention too," I say.

"See, he's got it handled," says Poppy, surveying the school. "It looks like a stand-up establishment, not a bad place to learn a few things."

"I don't like ties," I say.

"Lemme show you how it's done," says Poppy.

"I already showed him," says Nanna.

A moment of tension between them. I twist up my tie and nestle the knot beneath my collar. The way it presses against my neck is uncomfortable, restricting.

"You know, every kid's guardians come to the first day of school," says Poppy. "I bet they were all here, correct?"

"Yes," says Nanna. "They were."

"But how many of them come to the second day?" asks Poppy. "Only a select few."

"The ones who can't hold their liquor," says Nanna.

"Holding it's never been an issue," says Poppy. "It's the putting it down that's a challenge."

I chuckle. Poppy reaches to hold Nanna's hand, but she resists. Poppy turns his attention to me in the back seat. "So here we are," he says. "The second day of school. Some consider it more important than the first, because now you've got a day of experience under your belt. You've got the lay of the land. You know how to put your tie on, you know that you can multitask with the best of 'em, you've dipped your toes in the water."

He reaches into the back seat and yanks gently on my tie.

"I hate ties too," he says. "But there's a few ways to look at them. You can consider them leashes, with a student at one end and the school at the other. The principal has everyone by the balls, the same way a businessman's gotta follow his boss' orders. But for you, that's not the case. Ties are a different thing for you, because you're different. I mean, where's your backpack? No one else got the homework done before getting home, did they?"

I shake my head proudly.

Poppy slightly loosens my tie and unbuttons the top button of my shirt.

"Your tie is more like a one-sided leash. You're a dog with no owner. A smart dog, a wild hound, running free while the rest are tied down. But that comes with consequences. You don't want to just go crazy and bite the principal in the jugular, because then they'll notice your freedom. That's not a smart dog move. They'll call animal control. They'll toss you back in the kennel and lock you up."

"Sounds familiar," says Nanna.

"The key is to know you're free but keep it a secret for the most part," says Poppy.

"And how do I do that?" I ask.

"You'll figure it out," says Poppy. "That's half the fun."

"He's gunna be late if you keep rambling," says Nanna.

"Well, that would be fitting," says Poppy. "A free dog can't be held to a schedule."

"We'll see you later, Sweetie," says Nanna.

I say goodbye and exit the car.

Poppy flashes me a thumbs up out the window.

SUICIDE

One fascinating thing about suicide: It's the only endeavor in life which, by way of contemplating it but never doing it, you become more of an expert than someone who actually performs the act. Because the moment you gain an ounce of experience at the craft of suicide, you cease to know anything at all. You are gone. One might be tempted to say the same applies to death, but death is a process. Hence the term 'dying.' One is dying, then he dies. But we do not say that one is 'suiciding.' The distinction is an important one. Suicide is an act. It occurs in an instant. Death, however, unfolds. One can get a taste of death without dying. If a disease drags you to the verge of dying but you survive, you know more about death than your average person. You know more about death than a mortuary employee. Suicide is a different thing though. The real experts on the matter are the people who think long and hard about it but refrain from ever getting involved. As far as I know, it's the only case in which the critic is more knowledgeable than the artist. Tell me who knows more about suicide: the person who falls into one depression and shoots himself in the head at age twenty or the person who lives into his eighties and thinks about killing himself every day? There is, of course, the glaring question of failed suicide attempts. What if someone tries to kill himself and fails? Does he become more of an expert on the matter? One would hope. But he was certainly no virtuoso to begin with. If he'd put as much thought into it as I have, he'd have gotten the job done….

Chapter 14

It is not worth the bother of killing yourself, since you always kill yourself too late.
—Emil Cioran

I curled up in my blankets and tried not to think.

Maybe humans are inherently good, maybe we're bad. Maybe free will exists, maybe it doesn't. I don't see any evidence. Perhaps there is a God, probably not. None of it mattered. My hangover was all-world. Anything beyond that was none of my business.

I buried my face under a pillow. Sweating, shivering, hoping to be deleted. Many times in my life I've pondered suicide. It has usually been a philosophical exercise. In moments like these, though, the matter becomes more practical. Where is the eject button? Do you mind pointing me toward the basement? I'm ready to make a deal. Just tell me where to sign.

The sheets were soaked in sweat.

I imagined myself showing up at the gates of hell. The doorman asks for my name. He checks the list, then shakes his head. Confused, I request that he check again. I must be on there, I insist. He chuckles at me and explains that, like most people who show up at his gate, I don't quite understand the system. This is but the first basement. There are countless sub-basements beneath this, he says. Oh, wow, that's fascinating, I reply. So is hell the general term for all these basements or is it just what this first level is called? I can tell he finds me annoying. Hell is the term for whatever level is just beneath you, he says. I stand there pondering this news, then ask: Is there a bottom level? He shrugs.

He doesn't know. I think on it some more, then I ask: If every level is the hell of the level above it, is every level the heaven of the level below it? He grows perplexed. I repeat the question. As it turns out, the doorman has never heard of such a concept. What is this heaven you speak of? It's supposedly above reality, I explain, with reality itself being a kind of hell. He is mildly intrigued by this but goes on to explain that there's only one elevator on the premises, and earthly reality is the highest level, the penthouse. I weigh the ramifications of this, the fact that earth itself might be heaven. He interrupts my thoughts and asks me to move along. I'm holding up the enormous line. I insist that it doesn't matter, that a little extra wait doesn't mean much because we are all in this for eternity anyway. He smacks me in the face and has me escorted out by security. I try to continue my metaphysical inquisition, but the bouncers beat me to a bloody pulp with billy clubs and toss me into the elevator.

Down we go.

It's funny how all this works.

The bluebirds came and went.

I hated them.

I loved them.

I am them.

* * *

It was my own burial.

I was viewing the ceremony from high above, watching my casket being carried through a cemetery. A crowd was gathered. As the pallbearers neared my grave, my consciousness floated down into my body. And suddenly I was me again, lying there in the blackness of the casket, dead. The cushions lining the casket were plush. I had thought about this when Nanna and Poppy died: Those cushions inside caskets, they looked comfortable, more comfortable than a bed.

Was this a dream or a nightmare?

There I was, dressed in a magnificent suit, being lowered into the dirt, locked in a cozy little tomb. Archaeologists don't travel to Egypt to study tombs, I thought. There are billions of little tombs spread across the surface of our planet. What made the pharaohs so special was how much they were willing to dedicate to the interior decorating budget.

As the soil piled on top of my new home, I again exited my body and floated out of the grave. That's when I noticed that my pallbearers, all four of them, were Joseph A, each of them an exact replica of the others, wearing matching gray suits. And they were not sad or happy. They were entirely apathetic, just there to fulfill their duty of putting me into the ground. It was a job. Someone had to do it.

Then I scanned the crowd. They, too, were all Joseph A replicas. No friends were present, nor coworkers or relatives or old lovers. No Pancake or Gigi. No one. It was just a flock of Joey's, all of them indifferent to my passing. There was an honesty to this attitude, their detachment. It felt right, as though this was the proper way to say goodbye. No tears. No eulogy. There is no use standing around and delivering a speech on how to be buried and forgotten. We all learn the ropes eventually.

A drink suddenly appeared in everyone's hands. Every Joseph A had a flawless rum and ginger ale in his left hand, with the smoothest amber color and the perfect amount of ice. The whole herd lit up cigarettes. All at once, they raised their glasses, a toast to me.

"Live fast, die middle-aged," they said in unison.

But the way they said it.

It was in the wrong tone.

It was no motto.

It was a warning.

MONEY

People say money talks, and they're right. But they're typically referring to the influence that comes with possessing money, the power of having it. This constitutes a mere fraction of money's speaking engagements. Most of money's chatter is directed at the poor, at those who don't have it and probably never will. To these folks, money screams. It holds court in the slums and laundromats, in the warehouses and alleys. It targets the impoverished and weak. Money is a demagogue, a rabble-rouser, a prophet. Follow me, lowly peasants, and life will get better for you! Bow down to me! Pray to me! Make sacrifices in my name! Most of you will prove unworthy of me, but the holiest among you, the most committed, you will one day fill your pockets. Wealth will be yours. And only these saints, by way of acquiring me, will learn the truth: I provide the same thing that all other saviors bestow upon their faithful: nothing....

Chapter 15

To sell your soul is the easiest thing in the world.
—Ayn Rand

Cars and trucks jammed the 710 Freeway.

Realistically, if every person got out and walked, our speed would remain the same. The only change would be that we'd all get some exercise. The vehicles themselves served no purpose other than to burn gas. I could taste the pollution flooding in through the air conditioning vents.

Along the east side of the freeway, every good swath of land was taken up by homeless encampments. Most of these villages were newly incorporated. I knew this because when I used to make this drive daily, I always kept track of the real estate market. Plenty of development had happened over the past year or so. This area was being gentrified.

A group of roadside inhabitants was trying to roll an industrial refrigerator up a hill to their tent city. I thought about pulling off the road and offering to tow it behind my car. Now that's a job I could tolerate. What other services were lacking in this neck of the woods? How about being a mailman for these townships? I could create my own map of zip codes and offer a postal service that caters only to those outside of the traditional address system. We could pile the mail into Pancake's cart and—

I slammed on the brakes, skidding just short of the car in front of me. It was completely my fault. My entrepreneurial daydreams had distracted me. Nonetheless, I honked the horn. The horn is the most important part of a vehicle. Horsepower, leather interior, safety features, they're all irrelevant. The horn must be thunderous and punishing. It must be able to scream at the world in ways that I can't. So I spent some time doing that, honking at anyone who made the minutest of driving mistakes. Really I wasn't honking at them, the individuals. I was honking at society. These pathetic drivers were simply the front line, the foot soldiers of modernity.

The whole of today's American economy could be torn apart by just analyzing this stretch of highway before me. If there was a police checkpoint where each vehicle was stopped and asked the same series of questions, it would play out almost identically for every car. Here's how it would go for me:

"Your check engine light is on," says the cop.

I nod.

"Where are you going?"

"Work."

"Do you want to go to work?"

"No."

"Are you paid well?"

"Not really."

"Do you like your job?"

"No."

"How about your coworkers?"

"No."

"Have you been drinking?"

"Somewhat."

"What does somewhat mean?"

"A gallon of rum per day for about a year."

"I don't blame you."

"How about you? Do you like being a cop?"

"Don't test my patience."

What I really wanted to do was turn off the first exit and head to Hugh Two. It wasn't so much a ravenous craving for alcohol. It was an aversion to the system, a distaste for everything beyond the windshield. My personal system puts the American system to shame. And it requires minimal effort and planning. To shine within my system is very, very easy. All one needs is rum, ginger ale, and ice. You don't need a resume. You don't need a good attitude. You don't have to fake it. You can just be yourself. Yet there I was leaving my flawless arrangement, chasing money, reentering the despicable

American workforce, somehow considered the greatest commercial enterprise in human history.

I imagined myself doing this over and over and over again. Commuting, that's what they call it. Commuting is the practice of going from the place you want to be, commonly called home, to the place you don't want to be, commonly called work. You must work to survive. You go to work, you receive money, then you give some of that money back to the system to maintain things, such as this road. Oddly enough, though, each and every driver on this road wouldn't mind if an overpass collapsed, preferably causing catastrophic damage, thus allowing for all of us to remain home and fully avoid participation in the system.

Unfortunately, yes, this would create some work. Construction workers would have to rebuild the overpass. But everyone knows that construction workers don't really work. They just talk and eat sandwiches and smoke cigarettes and lean on shovels. The yellow vests, hardhats, and bulldozers are all merely props. But can we blame them? No. Of course they don't want to work. No one does. It's all part of the system. So take your time repairing that overpass, boys. Measure twice, cut once. Don't rush into anything. We're all looking forward to some time off.

* * *

I arrived at the office at 9:21am.

I said hello to my coworkers. Some were happy to see me back, others were not. Such was expected. Most of them I hated, a handful of them I was indifferent toward, and two of them I liked. This ratio of animosity to apathy to friendship is an intentional standard of corporate life. If you liked all of your coworkers, you wouldn't get anything done. If you hated all of them, you'd stop showing up. So the higher-ups must maintain a specific blend of relationships to keep you walking in the door. When you understand this, you stop trying to bond with your colleagues and accept that most of them, by design, are not your cup of tea. I myself never walk into any situation, especially a job, expecting to be fond of those around me. Only about twelve people, a few of them dead, have my stamp of approval.

"Welcome back," said David.

"Thanks for having me," I said.

"You're always welcome," he said.

"I appreciate it."

"What have you been up to?"

"Drinking rum, hanging out with the homeless."

He laughed. David is a good boss, one of my two comrades in the building. He appreciates the honesty. So much of what's said in an office, and life, is small talk, which is primarily lies. Small talk is so insignificant that the details can be swapped out for anything else. How was the weekend? It was good, it was bad, I took Judy to the movies, Daniel had a soccer game. None of it matters. Unless you dive into the specific failures and absurdity of your experience, your life might as well be the weather forecast. Sunny, cloudy, rainy. Who cares? You won't be going outside anyway. You're stuck in this fucking office all day.

"I woke up along the L.A. River about a month ago," I continued.

"Seriously?" asked David.

I nodded. I wasn't proud, nor was I being funny. I was just reporting on my life.

"Sounds rough," he said.

"Rough enough to end up back in here," I said.

Again, he laughed.

My desk was empty. In the year I'd been gone, they hadn't replaced me. My coffee mug was still on the desk, collecting dust. Right off the bat, this had me questioning my value to the company. I was either irreplaceable or completely unnecessary.

"Thank the Lord," said Harry, friend number two, as I sat down.

"There he is," I said.

We exchanged a handshake, a hug, some banter. "It's good to have some chatter going again," said Harry. "It's a damn library in here."

"That's disrespectful to libraries."

"Speaking of libraries, how's it going with the book?"

I had nearly forgotten: My reason for leaving this job in the first place had been to write a book. I told Harry it was moving along nicely, then changed the subject, asking him how things have been here in the office. He filled me in on some corporate drama. A few people had been fired, others hired, a workplace romance. None of it mattered in the slightest to me, so I kept asking questions. I wanted to get through an hour or two before even considering any actual work. But Harry cut me off ten minutes later. This was his typical move. He grows self-conscious about not being productive, looks around, then says: We should probably get back to work.

I always disagreed.

I spent a very long time, probably an hour, drinking a coffee in the kitchen area. Caffeine makes so much sense in an office. To commit to this kind of existence, to willingly return to misery each day, to know you're one of a billion people performing mindless tasks in the fluorescent sadness, requires pharmacological motivation. Look at these people, I thought, scanning all of the faces across the office. Most of these people I had almost successfully forgotten. I was so close. My brain had bagged them up and put them into the trash, ready to let them fade into obscurity. But here they were again, back in my life, and I in theirs.

It's criminal, really, how many humans we are forced to associate with in today's age. In ancient times, houses were for keeping out enemies, the dangerous others. Nowadays they're for keeping out people like this, the most common of citizens, people who would never in a million years hurt you but whose very lives make you consider ending your own.

Around 11:00, I started to analyze the irreplaceable vs. unnecessary situation. If this business had gone a year without me and was doing just fine, why was I being permitted to rejoin the company? Clearly I meant zero to the actual functioning of the company, because I didn't do anything. I was not productive. I could leave for a year or ten and the numbers wouldn't change.

But perhaps my value was that I represented a small fraction of everyone's psyche. Deep down, each employee longs to not care. They want to stroll in late, they want to be slackers, they want to make a mockery of the system. They wish their job was nothing to them. But they've let it become everything. That was my talent, perhaps—I tickled some forgotten neurons in each of their brains. I rekindled something they all felt at one time: Jobs should not exist. Everyone should quit. Within all laborers, including CEOs, there is a renegade, a madman, someone who wants to take a sledgehammer to the walls and laugh at the fact that anyone ever thought jobs were a solid idea.

Thus, I was honored to be the elected representative of the bad employee within each of our souls. I certainly held the torch for the most cancerous employee. There is no doubting that. But what must be taken into account is that the system itself, the entire structure of modern corporate life, is a cancer. It's a plague like nothing the world has ever seen. So, in a way, I was doing a great service. I was a cancer on the cancer. I was mutating, rebelling, doing my small part to kill the thing that's killing a few billion of us one shift at a time. Through this lens, I was a highly valuable member of the organization.

I took a two-hour lunch break.

At 2:07, I made a crucial decision. I had to quit. I had to leave this place. All the reasons I had left the job in the first place had already bubbled back up on day one: Commutes make no sense, offices are air-conditioned cages, desk jobs are the most effective method of eroding a soul, etc. Yes, I had cooked up the claim that I had value as the corporate archetype of youthful spirit, but that was a farce, a form of fun mental gymnastics I'd played in lieu of doing actual work. Realistically I provided nothing to the organization. In fact, if I'm a member of any group, it should not be eligible for the label of organization.

The next big question was whether to quit or get fired. I had already quit once, so the right thing to do was to seek termination. This would be an arduous task. I had already showed up twenty minutes late and admitted to the CEO that I recently woke up in a toxic riverbed, so the bar was set very high. Coming up with offenses to commit would turn into a job in and of itself. But I was here. I might as well be productive.

EMPLOYEES

There are three types of people who work American desk jobs. There are those who actually enjoy it, those who pretend to enjoy it, and those who openly hate it. The ones who hate it are the only sane group, the rational yet cancerous employees. We openly mock and laugh at the job, which typically leads to termination. The next group, the ones who truly enjoy it, a gross minority, have something closer to a mental illness, a delusion. They've let the voice of reason within them die completely, thus allowing themselves to feel true fulfillment in the act of eroding away at a desk for ten hours a day, completing tasks, clicking and typing, calling and selling, shipping and receiving. This outlook has echoes of a belief in an all-powerful God. It would be pleasant to be on that side of things, to exist as a rat in a cage and have no issue with it, to even see value in it. Unfortunately, the Creator did not bless me with such a mindset. The last group of employees, the ones who pretend to enjoy it, is the largest group. And they're the most interesting from a psychological perspective. They are living a life of cognitive dissonance. Their souls want out, but they continue to show up and put a smile on because they're told that this is just the way things go. How else is one to earn a living? The intriguing part about this group, though, is that eventually they must jump to one of the other two groups. They must either: (1) come to their senses and quit or, (2) concede to liking the job. There is no in-between. If you work the same job for twenty years and claim to hate it, is it really hate that you feel? No. Hate isn't the word for it. Toleration, that's what it is. And toleration is a form of love. You've put up with the job for two decades in the same way that one puts up with a mediocre spouse. The company has put a ring on you. It owns you. You file your taxes together....

Chapter 16

It only wanted to help me, dear little bird.
—John Fante

Even the commute became a celebration of life.

I sat in traffic blasting Frankie Miller and didn't honk once. Every commuter was a captive stuck in an automotive parade, breathing brake dust and listening to a sell-out radio host whose every word was a poorly hidden advertisement. How could I honk at any of these people? It would be like heckling people in a refugee camp. If anything, I wished to save these commuters. I wanted to put on my hazard lights and set up on the side of the highway with a sign: *REPENT! QUIT YOUR JOB HERE!*

Passengers would each receive a cigarette, some rum, and a brochure explaining the advantages of a nonexistent career path. Is there paid time off? Yes and no. We're always off, but it's unpaid. Are there benefits? Yes, mainly laughter and cynicism. Is there maternity leave? You can just bring the baby to the office. Mr. John doesn't check IDs. Does the company have a retirement plan? Don't worry, you won't live that long. Is there free lunch? The popcorn machine runs 24/7. I would taxi my new co-non-workers to Hugh Two, baptize them in the Sacred Sink, and begin indoctrination.

Welcome to the good life.

There is an entire world here outside the cave.

During my previous stint with the company, I was never what most would consider a reliable employee. I lacked structure. The only consistency about my routine was that I showed up late and left early. How late and how early? I couldn't say. We can't control all the variables. I just made sure to come in after everyone else and leave an hour or two after lunch. I could be counted on for that.

But once I was actually at the office, how I spent my time was always a total crapshoot. An office provides only so many options: peruse the internet, take my shirt off out in the parking lot and get some sun, enjoy a snack break, lurk by the coffee maker for a few hours, pester some coworkers, read a book, take my lunch break, nap in my car, go for a walk for an hour or two, slip away to the bar around the block, smoke cigarettes out back, or do work. Typically, I would perform actual work for around thirty or forty minutes a day if I was firing on all cylinders. This was rare and required copious amounts of caffeine, but it did happen.

But all of this changed once I became a chosen employee. Counterintuitively, the choice to quit brought about routine. I discovered the rhythms of a company man. It was clockwork. Every day of that glorious week, I arrived at the office about an hour late, downed two cups of coffee, talked to Harry for thirty minutes, then went into the bathroom. I did in fact need to use the bathroom, but I opted to extend my stay in the stall for an absurd amount of time.

The first day I brought my cell phone in there with me. This was a tactical error: Harry had to use the stall and called me. I was forced to pick up because he was standing outside the stall, listening to my phone ring, and coming up with mock voicemail messages: "I can't get to the phone right now, I've been in the restroom for forty-five minutes." I couldn't help but laugh. I'll be out in a minute, I told him. You know how it goes. This office coffee really moves the bowels.

The following day I cleaned up my act and left my phone out on my desk. Obviously, everyone knew it was me in the stall, but it was baffling how hesitant people were to knock. Even Harry didn't dare to bother me because he couldn't be entirely sure that it was me in there. If he peeked over the stall and it turned out to be another employee, that would be sexual harassment in the state of California. As a general guideline, pretty much everything is harassment in the state of California. You cannot mock coworkers, you cannot flirt with coworkers, you cannot even look at a coworker in a mocking or flirtatious way. That crosses most of life off the list. To not harass someone in a liberal state, you must essentially forfeit every fiber of your humanity.

Instead of outlawing everything, it would be easier to just center the laws around the things you *can do* in workplaces. This would be the environmental move too, saving boatloads of paper, because the document would be one sentence long: *You're permitted to work.*

By Friday, I really hit my stride. Instead of going right into the bathroom, I exited the front door of the office as if taking a phone call. At my car, I switched into different shoes, some of Poppy's old loafers, a pair of shoes I would never myself wear, then reentered the office through the back door. Into the stall I went. I was in there for so long that a few people peered under the stall door, clear cases of sexual harassment, but the shoes worked like a charm. No one knew who the bathroom bandit was. I sat in there for at least two hours. This time frame was an estimate, of course. My only gauge on the clock was counting how many times the motion-sensing light would click off and leave me sitting there in the dark. Then I would wave my hand. *Click!* The fluorescent sadness would again conquer the bathroom.

Light is so often associated with good, with purity, but fluorescent light is a different thing. It is the color of emptiness. If one day the sun, by some bizarre chemical reaction, a solar midlife crisis, began emitting fluorescent light, that would be the end of it all. The whole of our planet would be turned into an office. Initially there would be some novelty about it. Look, there's trees in the office, entire forests. But the trees would all die. Not to worry, there's mountains too. It's so nice to get outside like this. But within a few weeks, the fluorescent sadness would kick in. It gets to us all. And eventually we would all do what was necessary: mass suicide. *Click!* A planet gone dark.

"Everything okay in there?" asked Pat.

I said nothing and faked a low grunt of abdominal distress. Pat was widely known as the worst person in the office. He possessed all of the annoying coworker traits: He enjoyed the job, he took things very seriously, he looked down on anyone who made less money than he did, he successfully schemed for corporate power, and he rooted his identity in career success. Beyond that, he was a generally unlikable human being.

Pat did, however, without his knowledge, have some upside: He was a key source of employee bonding. He was like the USSR during the Cold War: If an awkward silence hit near the water cooler, it didn't matter if you were talking to a janitor or a software engineer, you could always express contempt for Pat as a fallback and the conversation would be rekindled.

Pat's key flaw was that he had zero respect for human corruption. Such a trait requires an unthinkable level of arrogance. The only way to achieve this is to assume you're infallible, thus blinding yourself to your own flaws, which prohibits you from seeing a little bit of yourself in all the fucked up happenings of our species. This being the case, he didn't find any comedy in my bathroom shenanigans. He saw it as pure laziness.

All I wanted was for someone to walk into the bathroom, shake my hand, and tell me that it was hilarious and bold to sit in the stall for twenty-four motion-sensing light cycles. Is that too much to ask?

"Excuse me," Pat persisted, knocking on the stall door.

I unlocked the door, exited, and realized I had to use the bathroom. I unzipped my fly and set up shop at the urinal.

"Other people need to use the bathroom too," he said.

"A spokesman for the people," I said.

"You've been in here for two hours."

"That was my guess too," I said.

I had made it to lunchtime.

* * *

The bells jingled as I swung open the door.

"He is not dead," said Amir.

"Getting there," I said.

"You have been taking your business elsewhere?"

"I haven't been doing business," I said. "Well, technically, I have. Just the wrong kind of business. I've been doing actual business, like at a job."

Amir laughed.

I'd never heard him laugh before. He laughed so hard that I laughed with him. But then he just kept laughing, cackling away. Was the idea of me having a job really that hilarious? I guess so. He repeatedly slammed his hand down on the countertop, gasping for air like I'd told the greatest joke he'd ever heard. So I left him there, laughing and mocking my life, to gather what I'd come for.

The bottle was just as I'd remembered. I appreciated its handle, its shape, its gentle curves catching the light. Every one of these bottles has an identical shape, and yet its main characteristic is uncertainty. That's why I was here. My physical withdrawal symptoms were gone. I felt decent enough. I wasn't here for the alcohol itself. I came to reacquaint myself with the unknown. If done right, to drink is to poison oneself with uncertainty.

Sometimes this uncertainty is fun and manageable. It's uncontrollable laughter, utter invincibility. Other times it's gruesome and overwhelming. It's hell and some ice cubes. But such is the bargain between the drinker and the drink, an arrangement no different than any other game worth playing. There is a winner and a loser. Every now and again the drink hoists the trophy.

In taking such an approach to alcohol, one can easily answer the timeless question: Do I have a drinking problem? Well, if you consistently lose the game, then, yes. You have a problem. If the question makes you feel uneasy, like you'd rather not address it, which is very much the sensation I had as I grabbed the bottle of rum, then you also might have a problem. So long as you can convince yourself it's still a game, though, it remains bearable. This is true for both drinking and life.

I set my bottle of rum on the counter and waited as Amir restocked some scratch-off tickets. Standing there and watching him work, I realized this was his office. He commuted here, he flipped on these lights every morning, he mopped the floors, he scraped money together to make ends meet. I am sorry, Amir. If I had the money, I would give it to you.

Most people think about money as a tool to acquire things. But it's really not about what you would do with wealth. It's about what you wouldn't do. That's the greatest value of money: the freedom to not do certain things.

If Amir were to hit it big on one of those scratch-off tickets and win fifty million dollars, his purchase of a yacht would not be as gratifying as his first day at home, lounging on the couch, not selling liquor to the insatiable mob. Flying first class back home to India to visit his parents wouldn't soothe his soul as much as permanently flipping that OPEN sign on the door to CLOSED, knowing he'd never deal with someone like me again. Not having a job is far greater than having anything.

Our society seems irrationally terrified by the thought of unemployment. Politicians rant about the dangers of joblessness, the horrors of a life without purpose. But if we're going to concoct a purpose to life, to lie to ourselves and insist this whole game has an underlying meaning, is a job really the best we can do? We're better than that. Personally, I'd love for a politician to step up and vow to solve the employment problem. That candidate would have my vote. Employment is the greatest human blunder.

"Some supplies for your job, I see," chuckled Amir.

"I really do have a job," I said, handing him $22 I borrowed from Harry.

"Oh, yes, a working man now, very good," he sneered. "Enjoy your day off."

"I'm on the clock," I told him, knocking over the tip jar as I left.

I was urged not to return.

* * *

I heard Pancake and Lana screaming at each other as I ascended the stairs.

Once up on the bike path, I had a proper vantage point of the Ravine. Lana, standing just outside the tent, was throwing rocks at Pancake who was using his shopping cart as cover, launching return fire. Lana's accuracy was remarkable. Rocks peppered the shopping cart and made it impossible for Pancake to make a move. He occasionally put both hands up in surrender, but Lana was having none of it. She continued to bombard him.

I sat down to enjoy the show.

Eventually Lana called in the big guns. She found an enormous rock and, using both hands, hucked it toward Pancake. It smashed into his cart, knocking it over on top of him. For a moment, there was silence. I thought Pancake was done for. But then he let out one of his wolf howls and wiggled his way out from beneath the cart. He glared and pointed at Lana, his arm shaking with fury. "If it broke, you're mincemeat!" he screamed.

"Good luck with that," Lana said calmly.

My guess was that Pancake was worried about the cart itself. He lifted it upright and rummaged through its contents. Deep in the bottom of his stash, he pulled out something oblong, wrapped in a psychedelic tapestry. He felt the item for breaks. It was unscathed. As Pancake let out a sigh of relief and hugged the object, Lana resumed fire. A small rock caught Pancake on the side of the head. Out came another wolf's howl.

"Howdy," I said.

My hope was that my presence would facilitate a ceasefire. But within seconds, Lana was launching rocks at me too. If I had been feeling martial, this would have been a mistake on her part: I had the higher ground.

"I surrender! I surrender!" I shouted.

The bombardment didn't stop until Pancake came to my aid. He hit Lana square in the chest with a piece of driftwood and down she went, then he came scrambling up the embankment with his precious gadget and sprinted past me.

"This way, Sarge!" he screamed.

"Copy!" he responded. "Take cover beyond the treeline!"

We hightailed out of there.

There were no trees.

SELF-DESTRUCTION

Sadness can just show up in your bed. You never invited her over. You can't kick her out. She might leave next Thursday. She might stick around forever. And this nonsensical nature of despair, the fact that the deepest sorrow can hit you without the slightest warning, is one of the root causes of self-destruction. We want to paint our illogical gloom with reason. We want the pain to make sense, for it to fit into the neat world of cause and effect. So we run headfirst into mistakes and destroy ourselves, because we want to mark it on the calendar: Yes, see that right there? That made me sad. It's a futile attempt at tethering our timeless woes to the temporal. The world cuts deep. Sometimes it's nice to hold the knife....

Chapter 17

...if he suffered a loss, he laughed and said,
'Oh well, this transaction has gone badly.'
—Herman Hesse

Pancake was playing with all the dials in my car, toggling between radio stations, opening the glove compartment, activating the windshield wipers.

"What is that?" I asked.

"It turns on the wipers," he said.

"No, I mean that thing." I gestured to his sacred item.

"Oh," he said. "Don't mind if I do." He ceremoniously unwrapped the article very slowly, humming Beethoven's Fifth Symphony, to reveal a yellow lava lamp.

"Damn," I said.

"Yeah," he said.

"Where did you get it?"

"The antique shop on Pine."

"You steal it?" I asked.

"They gave it to me in exchange for services rendered."

"What services?"

"I exposed a security breach for them," he said.

"A chink in the armor, my lord!" he sang out the window.

"I smashed the front window with a lawn chair," he explained.

He kissed the lava lamp, whispered something to it, re-swaddled it with the tapestry, then strapped it into the back seat with a seatbelt.

"What's Lana so mad about?" I asked.

"The shoe," said Pancake.

"It's still missing?"

"Goner than the wind."

"We must have hid that thing very well," I said.

"We know what we're doing," he said.

I offered him a fist pound, but he opened up my fingers and firmly shook my hand. A minute later I had to pry myself free.

"I can buy her a new pair of shoes," I offered.

"That's not allowed."

"But if it's actually gone this time, like gone gone, we might have to."

"It'll turn up," said Pancake.

We drove for fifteen minutes before he even asked where we were going. I broke down the situation for him: I was back at my job. Since it was the second Friday of the month, the company hosts a casual office happy hour for employees and friends. I wanted him to join. First, he mocked me for having a job and briefly considered jumping out of the moving vehicle. Then he asked why he should help me out after I had, during my brief wave of sobriety, ignored his knocks on my front door. He had showed up twice, he said, once to microwave some clothes and another time to fill me in on the Joseph A situation, and I hadn't answered the door. I apologized and accepted my mistakes. That didn't help much. So I poured him some rum and informed him that I would be quitting the job. He congratulated me.

"That's one good part about a job," I said. "You've gotta have one to quit."

Loving this statement, Pancake rubbed his hands together giddily and tried to smack me in the face. I blocked it, so he simply rubbed my belly and said, "Rain."

"Speaking of Joseph A," I said. "Everyone in my office is pretty much a Joey-boy, but you have to understand that there are levels to it."

"Joseph A equals Joseph B," said Pancake.

"Sort of," I said. "But some are worse than others. A few of them aren't terrible."

"One week and they've got you brainwashed," he said.

"I'll be the judge of that!" he cried.

Then, using his hands as a megaphone: "Quiet on the set!"

When I told him there would be free alcohol and sandwiches, he licked his lips for a while, a dozen or so revolutions. Then he asked if any of the sandwiches would be chicken parmesan. I told him I wasn't sure, but that it wasn't out of the question.

"The office got a pool table?" he asked. "La mesa de billar."

"No," I said.

"How about gaspers? You can smoke in offices, correct?"

I presumed Pancake's mind was swimming with images of American corporate life in the 1960s when men in suits chain-smoked cigarettes and sexually harassed all of the female employees. Smoking in our office, however, was strictly forbidden. I assured him it was allowed.

He clapped.

*　*　*

We parked out front.

Through the windows, I could see that the happy hour was underway. About fifteen coworkers, along with some friends and spouses, were gathered in the lounge area of the office, standing around and engaging in mild conversation. They all looked presentable, like they earned fifty thousand dollars or more annually: the recipe for a bad party.

Poor people are the soul of a good party. Or a good neighborhood. The peasants have nothing to lose. They bring the flavor. Causing mayhem or embarrassing themselves is of no concern. There is no job to lose, no fortune to squander. Thus the party, and the poverty cycle, continues.

I'm ashamed to confess that I used to appreciate these lame office parties. My procedure was to drink twelve to fifteen beers, pressure coworkers to join me at a nearby shithole bar, then head off to that bar alone and ingratiate myself with the local proletariat.

"What's this we've got here?" asked Pancake, staring into the office.

"That's the happy hour," I said. "This is where I work."

Pancake was bewildered. He got out of the car and approached the windows, peering in through the glass. Everyone inside spotted him and stared back, whispering to each other, wondering if he was going to smash the glass with a rock.

I joined him at the window.

"What are they doing?" asked Pancake.

"This is how they party."

"Why?" he asked.

"I don't know," I said.

Everyone waved to Pancake. He waved back, then grabbed his swaddled lava lamp from the back seat of the car. "I'll be needing power," he said.

In we went.

The room went so silent that you could hear the air conditioning units. Pancake did an army salute to no one in particular, then beelined to the spread of sandwiches. He set aside the lava lamp before rigorously inspecting the sandwiches, making sure they were up to code.

"He's a friend of yours?" asked David.

I nodded.

"Who's your buddy?" asked Harry, joining us.

"He goes by Pancake," I said.

Harry held back a smirk. I had told him earlier in the week about the friendship I'd developed with Pancake. The three of us watched as Pancake examined the sandwiches. He pulled the top piece of bread off each one, analyzed the layers of meat and cheese and lettuce, then, once disappointed, haphazardly tossed the top piece of bread aside. Most of the bread fell onto the floor, some pieces landed on the table, and a few he slipped into his pockets. He lobbed one slice of bread into the air, and, by sheer luck, it settled right back onto the lower half of one of the sandwiches. He threw his arms up in celebration. "Kambooma!" he screamed, glancing around to see if anyone witnessed it.

I saw it, as did Harry. We both gave him a thumbs up.

Eventually he made his way to the cooler of craft beers and rifled through them, again disappointed by the options. The other employees who were congregated in the vicinity slowly dispersed. They weren't rude about it, but they made sure to distance themselves from him. Pancake settled on three different beers, slipped two into his waistline, and joined us.

"Thanks for coming," David said to him.

"Do you mind?" asked Pancake, gesturing to an outlet.

"Not at all," said David, unsure of what Pancake even meant.

Pancake retrieved his lava lamp, got down on his hands and knees, and cautiously unwrapped it from the tapestry. Next, he folded the tapestry and, for reasons unknown, handed it to Shawna, the wife of a coworker. She placed it on the sandwich table. Pancake then carried the lava lamp over to the outlet and plugged it in. He stepped back to admire it for a moment and froze, mesmerized by its magnificent yellow glow.

"Pancake," I said.

He snapped out of it and approached David. "You the head honcho here?"

"That I am," said David. "The name's David." He offered a handshake.

Before accepting, Pancake looked David up and down. He did a full lap around him, sizing up everything about him. Apparently David passed the test because Pancake respectfully shook his hand and said, "Tell me about your business model."

Taken aback, David gave a three-minute breakdown of the company. His description was spot-on. It was concise, insightful, and not too jargon-heavy. He boiled it down in a way that anyone with a brain could understand.

"You need chicken parmesan," responded Pancake.

We all chuckled, but Pancake wasn't horsing around. He took two of the bread slices out of his pockets and demonstrated to David why chicken parm was superior to all other sandwiches. "The melted cheese," he stressed. "It holds it all together, creates solidarity."

"I'm a chicken parm guy myself," Harry chimed in.

This prompted Pancake to give Harry the same treatment that he gave David: heavy scrutiny, lapping him and analyzing, muttering to himself. Harry, too, passed his evaluation. Pancake shook his hand then explained that he was going to clear the perimeter and check for vulnerabilities. He disappeared into the office area.

"How'd you meet this character?" asked David.

"I'm not even sure," I said.

"I hope you don't mind me asking," said David. "But is he of sound mind?"

"No," I said, taking a pull of rum.

David eyed the flask.

"Rum," I clarified, then took off to check on Pancake in the office area. I was worried that he might, due to their connection with the internet, smash the computers. But it appeared he had restrained himself. Everything was intact. Where was Pancake? I found it hard to believe he wasn't bolting around in the fluorescent sadness, pressing keyboards and clicking mouses to see what kind of soundscape corporate America provided. I checked the conference room next. Maybe he was holding a meeting with himselves. No, he was not. Nor was he bathing in the bathroom sink.

I finally located him being shockingly tame in the kitchen area. Brewing himself a coffee, he was stuffing as many wooden coffee stirrers into his pockets as possible.

"What are you going to use those for?" I asked.

"Something will emerge," he said.

He lit up a cigarette. I was glad that he chose the kitchen to smoke because it was the one area in the office with a slew of California Labor Law posters on the wall, all of which had *NO SMOKING* in bold print. I lit one up for myself. It was time to get the ball rolling.

The two of us hung out alone in the kitchen for a while and got obliterated, smoking cigarettes and eating snacks that other employees had stored in the fridge. We downed a whole six-pack of organic yogurt, then did away with a tub of peanut butter.

Eventually, Pat came in.

"What's going on in here?" he asked.

Pancake immediately recognized Pat as a high-ranking Joseph A. It was an amazing display of intuition. Without saying a word, Pancake approached Pat and circled, surrounding him with a ring of smoke. Pat frantically waved away the smoke, coughing and squinting as if a few secondhand puffs meant stage four lung cancer.

"Is he with you?" asked Pat.

I nodded.

"You guys can't smoke in here," said Pat.

Pancake lifted the collar on the back of Pat's button-down shirt, checking underneath the flap. I don't know what would've possibly been under there, but he was just being thorough. This was the final straw: Pat had failed the inspection. Pancake calmly grabbed an open beer off the counter, walked over to Pat, and went to pour it over his head.

"Don't even think about it," said Pat, backing away. Pancake opted to pour the beer onto Pat's left shoulder. "What's your problem, man!" yelled Pat, shimmying out of the way. But Pancake stayed with him, emptying the beer, soaking Pat's whole left side in beer.

"You're done here, you know that!" Pat screamed at me.

I nodded.

"Joey-boy!" belted Pancake inches from Pat's face, raining saliva onto him. Livid, Pat wiped himself down with a paper towel then disappeared to tattle on us.

"That was good," I said.

"I must when I must," said Pancake.

"Ask and you shall receive!" he sang like a Catholic priest.

"Now, now, Sarge," he said, wagging his finger at himself. "We've gotten ourselves into a good ole donnybrook here."

David curiously poked his head into the kitchen. Spotting the smoke and the mess we'd made, he looked at me with utter disappointment. I really did feel bad because David had never been anything but nice to me. I should have never been hired in the first place, let alone permitted to work at the company twice. But if I was going to be fired, I had to do it the right way. My only hope was that he respected the initiative, the fireworks of it all.

Beep! Beep! Beep! Beep!

Pancake shuffled over to the microwave and swung it open.

The room instantly smelled of burning textiles, a charred mustiness. Pancake checked the drawers for utensils or an oven mitt. No luck. Then he turned to me and raised his eyebrows, knowing I would appreciate his prophetic call. He slid two wooden coffee stirrers out of his pocket. "Greetings, Chairman Mao," said Pancake to the stirrers. Using them as chopsticks, he plucked his steaming socks from the microwave. "Microbes," he explained to David.

Then, as David watched with curiosity, Pancake deposited his socks in the refrigerator to cool them down. Next, he began wiping his dirty feet with paper towels and dish soap. As he did so, clearing away the filth, he said to David, "I used to work in a place like this."

"It that right?" said David.

"I wouldn't call it right," said Pancake. "But it's something I've come to live with."

"What kind of company?"

"Who cares?" asked Pancake.

"Entirely irrelevant!" he sang in self-support.

Then Pancake continued as he put his socks back on: "Asking what a company sells, that's like asking what the cause of death was in a homicide, boss. Is there a good way to kill? No, no! There's no good way to murder!" He began hopping on one foot, struggling to get his left sock back on, his rage swelling. Finally, he slipped on his sock and began cornering David, walking him down. "The same goes for selling things! Murder and sales, brothers in arms! You've got plenty of good salesmen out there, yes, David! You've got a whole office of killers!"

David slowly retreated into a corner, and I did not blame him. Pancake was stalking him, his muscles tensing, a foreboding scowl on his face. I was worried that the homicidal theme may have taken root in his mind, that he was about to strangle David to death and do away with what he considered just another figurehead of the capitalist machine.

Instead, though, Pancake grabbed David's hand and kissed it gently. "My lord, how good it must feel to have killers on the payroll!" Then he rushed out into the office area and went wild. He began demolishing everything in sight: chairs, computers, desks, fans. He raced around in circles. He tossed stacks of paper into the air. He ripped wires out of the walls. He sang Frankie Miller. He jumped up on desks. He stomped on keyboards. He embodied madness.

David turned to me calmly: "Why?" While distressed, he maintained the composure of a leader, a CEO.

"Sorry," I said.

"You knew he would do this?"

"No."

"But you knew he would do something."

I didn't know what to say, so I exited the building. Once alone outside, I let out a bluebird call. I squawked to the heavens.

Are there any of you nearby?

I believe I have made a mistake.

* * *

As we drove down the 710 Freeway, there was tension between myself and Pancake. This tension was also playing out within me: I didn't know whether to congratulate him or scream at him. On the one hand, I was in awe of his destruction of the office. It was miraculous. Every employee in every office in America, at least once per day, dreams of such a thing. But to see it actually carried out, to watch Pancake lay waste to everything, it hurt something in me.

To people like us, offices are indeed atrocious. They're prisons. But to many others, most of them decent enough humans, offices are second homes. They are places to earn a living and meet new people and feel a sense of purpose. It's not their fault that our society has, for some god-forsaken reason, made the fluorescent sadness a focal point of life. They can't help it. They're just doing what they must. And the decimation of that office felt like harming all of those poor employees trapped in that building, all of those faces I used to see every day. To not feel kinship with someone is one thing. To harm him is another.

After all, we need the common man. We need offices. Things need to be accomplished. Food and goods and medical supplies and gasoline need to be shipped. Lives depend on it. I was not blind to this fact, nor was Pancake. The issue was that the necessity of it, the irrefutable fact that the economy needed to be maintained at all costs, made us sick to our stomachs. It was set in stone. It required conformity. It was a silencing of the animal.

But if conformism was removed from the collective human psyche, the rebel, too, would die. What would there be to rebel against? The rebel needs the herd. Consequently, if one fancies himself a rebel, he should have at least some gratitude for the lack of individuality among most people, because it is a prerequisite for his own individuality.

Weaving through traffic, I accepted this. I silently thanked each driver I passed. Keep up the good work, my fellow citizens. You are critical to the function of our economy. Each and every one of you is making a great sacrifice. The world needs people like you. But, far more importantly, I need people like you, for you must exist for me not to be you.

I had to cut off this train of thought. Because the arrogance, the selfishness of it, shook me to the core. It also lacked originality. Yes, the outlier needs the crowd, genius. In fact, to even have such a thought makes you part of a crowd, a crowd of idiots who had the very same idea and thought it was original. Roll down the window and stop thinking, I told myself. And I did so. But as I let the polluted Los Angeles wind hit my face, a shiny luxury car pulled up beside me in the left lane. Driving it was an older man, a company man in his sixties, donning a navy blue suit and tie, his hair sculpted with gel. I waited for him to glance my way, but he never did. He only stared ahead, a soullessness about him, as though it didn't matter which way he looked. They were all the same thing.

Life hurts for that man too, I reminded myself.

You know this.

As a rule, an unbreakable rule, life finds a way to hurt. There's no way around it. As for what form the pain comes in, that's up to fate. But pain will indeed be served. Prepare the table.

Look at that poor man.

Conformity hurts just as bad as rebellion.

Must you see more?

My heart bled for that man. It bled and it bled. And the blood spoke to me. It said this: You are more similar to that man than you are dissimilar to him. Admit it, you fool. Let your guard down. You and him, like all of humanity, are lost and hurting and dying and ardently committed to acting otherwise. That man has his ways, his expensive car and his suit and tie, and I have mine. But the fight is one and the same.

Life itself is a matter of palliative care. To exist successfully is to properly manage the pain. The best anyone can do is get comfortable. Kick the shoes off. Pour yourself a drink. Laugh your way into the dirt. It will be so nice and quiet underground.

"You didn't have to do that," I said to Pancake.

"Zapping the microbes," he said. "It's all—"

"I'm talking about destroying the office," I snapped.

"Oh, yes," said Pancake. "There are other ways it could have happened."

Pancake did let out a sigh, the subtlest of regrets. But minutes later he forgot about the whole thing. I chose to move on from it as well, because I knew that it was largely my fault. I had taken a madman into an office, a place that can drive the sanest of men mad. I was lucky Pancake hadn't killed someone or set fire to the building. All we could hope for now was that insurance would cover the damages. And that David wouldn't pursue legal action. I realized also that I'd made a strategic error: I should have at least worked two weeks before tearing it all down. That way I would have gotten my first paycheck.

Pancake broke a long silence: "If we're lucky, Joey-boy'll show again tonight."

"At Hugh?"

Pancake nodded with fire in his eyes.

"He came back?" I asked.

"How many times must I explain? The man's a lifeguard. He'll keep coming back and coming back as long as drowning exists."

He hollered in a female voice: "There are devils in the deep!"

Then he resumed: "The coward barricaded himself in the bathroom and snuck off while I was getting myself established in the Beauty." He pulled out a coffee mug he stole from the office and poured himself some rum.

"You come away with anything else?" I asked.

Out came some bread, the coffee stirrers, two staplers, a mouse pad, a few dozen pens and pencils, a keyboard, scissors, rubber bands, and a bundle of wires made up mostly of extension cords. Then he reached down the leg of his pants and unsheathed a long metal three-hole punch machine, holding it up like a sword.

"Men are wretched things," he said.

He sliced and diced the air for a minute but got tired of it. Then he started striking the dashboard, denting it, and unsuccessfully trying to jab his lance into the A/C vents.

"What kind of magic is this?" he asked, not knowing what a three-hole punch was.

Whoop! Whoop!

Blue lights flashed from behind us.

"Blueys," said Pancake casually.

I did my best to stay calm, slowing my breathing as I pulled off onto the side of the road. What was this about? I had been driving normally, doing the speed limit. Had David called the cops and given them my information?

Pancake obliviously went to pour himself another cup of rum.

"Hide that!" I shouted.

I heard footsteps approaching. Slow, purposeful footsteps. I imagined it being Officer Nellins. He'd make a snarky comment about how this encounter was meant to be, how he knew in his heart of hearts that he would see me again and make me suffer.

"License and registration," said the officer.

As I pulled out my wallet, the officer leaned down into the window and stared toward the passenger seat. I glanced in the same direction. The bottle was sitting on Pancake's lap, the coffee mug in his hand. He raised the drink in salute as if nothing about it was illegal and said, "Hello, scum."

"Have you been drinking?" the officer asked me.

I hesitated, scrambling for excuses, but lying would only delay the inevitable. I told him the truth: "A gallon of rum per day for about a year."

"Rain," said Pancake.

I had been pulled over for a broken taillight. Both Pancake and I were arrested, my car impounded. My charge was DWI. My registration was expired too. Pancake willingly confessed to having about two and half miles worth of methamphetamine in his left shoe. He was unfazed by any of it.

Once we were in handcuffs in the back of the police cruiser, I realized the nature of our miscommunication, why Pancake hadn't concealed the rum.

"Are there any weapons in the vehicle?" asked the officer.

"Under my seat there's a little something to wet your whistle," said Pancake. He had stashed the three-hole punch.

* * *

We were locked in a holding cell overnight.

Six other people were in there with us, two of whom Pancake knew. One of them was an emaciated woman named Bunny. She said that the female holding cell, normally a separate chamber, was being cleaned out after someone gave birth in it. Bunny and Pancake seemed to go way back. She rubbed his feet, he scratched her back, and they discussed the crimes of their past. At one point, she tried to reach down his pants, but he informed her that he had a woman at home.

Another detainee was a man named Bam-Bam Barry. He was six-foot-five and had a tattoo that read *THE WORLD IS MINE* across his throat. While he and Pancake were friendly, Pancake warned me to tread lightly. He'd once seen Bam-Bam Barry beat someone to death with a washing machine. I had trouble picturing how one would go about this, which made it all the more scary.

The guards brought each of us a pathetic cheese sandwich.

Before I could even take a bite, Bam-Bam Barry pointed at me. He didn't have to say a word. I knew what he wanted. While I was starving, I also valued my life. I gave Bam-Bam Barry my cheese sandwich.

Then, in what began as a discussion about Richard Nixon's hair, Pancake and Bam-Bam Barry got into an argument about whether or not the Vietnam War was justified. Pancake claimed it was. This prompted Bam-Bam to label Pancake as a racist, but Pancake vehemently denied the accusation. There was no way he could be racist, he said, because he hated the majority of his own race as well. He assured Bam-Bam Barry that he never judged anyone by their skin color or gender or *what flavors they liked to fuck.*

Eventually Pancake carved out his primary theme: Racism was, in fact, a stupid form of hatred because it was too limited. Referencing Martin Luther King, he claimed that, in judging people strictly on the quality of their character, one could hate at a far higher rate than any racist ever could. It was a visionary outlook. I'd never summarized my personal platform on hatred, but this was a close match.

I seconded Pancake's point, voicing a thought I'd once developed in John F. Kennedy airport: Racists are very much like the people who throw a fit when their flight gets delayed, the morons who vow to never fly with an airline again because of a single mistake. Clearly such folks are not seasoned travelers. If they were, they'd know that the difference between airlines is very much like the difference between races: There is no difference. Given enough chances, all of them will find a way to disappoint you. Just keep traveling, keep meeting people. You will learn this. Thankfully, though, disappointment is hilarious. There is plenty of laughter on the itinerary.

My theory was well-received.

"Rain," agreed Pancake. Bunny touched my thigh. Bam-Bam Barry, however, didn't buy it yet. Eyes locked on mine, he slowly approached, rubbing his hands together. He leaned uncomfortably close to my face, his whiskey breath burning my eyes. I assumed that he was about to beat me to death. I glanced around the cell. What would be his weapon of choice? If he was a thinking man, he could turn Bunny into the murder weapon. Grab her by the feet and swing her around. She was frail and likely hadn't eaten in weeks, but her head would do the job. They say the human head weighs eight pounds. Instead, though, Bam-Bam Barry placed both of his hands on my shoulders and asked: "Do you hate?"

I nodded.

He nodded in return, squeezing my shoulders. Bam-Bam Barry believed me. He believed that there was indeed hate in my heart. And it didn't seem to matter to him whether I hated an entire race or licorice or the Boston Red Sox. Any hate was good in his book.

A few hours later, Officer Nellins came strolling by, finishing a shift. He took a quick look into the cell, giving Bam-Bam Barry a cordial nod of the head. I tried to catch his glance, but he paid me no mind. I was just another person in the cell.

"Granola man," said Bam-Bam Barry as Nellins disappeared.

Five minutes later Officer Nellins arrived with seven granola bars, one for each of us. The other prisoners seemed to know who he was: the cop who brought granola bars to everyone in the holding cell. My initial theory was that the only reason Officer Nellins did such a thing was to assert power over us, to subtly hint that he controlled our destiny. But I did my best to view the situation in its most basic terms: There are seven hungry animals, and another animal brings them food. Could there be evil in such a thing? Perhaps. But with enough cynicism, evil can be mined from any action.

Nellins even stuck around for a short conversation, asking Bam-Bam Barry about his wife and kids. Bam-Bam Barry informed Nellins that he'd caught his wife having sex with his uncle, but that they'd moved beyond that. Everything was perfect now. His kids were still alive.

I ate my granola bar and laid down on the cold concrete between Bunny and Pancake. Animals sleep on the floor.

FIRE

Something is certainly on fire, but it has become very difficult to track the flames. It's tough to see through all this smoke. It burns the eyes. Is the world ablaze? Or is it just my life? Does the cynic have a keen nose for smoke? Or is he holding the torch? Another classic manifestation of the chicken and the egg. Regardless, though, we have a fire on our hands. Things are burning. These words are the ashes....

Chapter 18

After two days I walked out of jail like a dying man.

It was a hot, dry morning, the sun vicious and unforgiving. I needed food, I needed water, and I needed a drink. My hangover was of the all-world variety. But from a psychological perspective, there was a weightlessness about things, a levity. I had thrust myself into unavoidable forward motion. I had backed myself into a corner. The boats had been set ablaze. No longer was it possible to return to my job. Nor could I carry on living as I had been living for the past year or so, for that way of life had led me here, penniless and squinting on the marble steps of the police station as the rest of the city drank their coffee and soldiered on against it all.

The future awaited me. As for what it held, I hadn't the slightest idea. But is that not the purest form of future? The less known a future is, the more of a future it is. If a future is too easily foreseen, that means it is too tied to the past, too much an offspring of what once was, like a child who too closely impersonates his parents. What use is there getting to know a reproduction? I'd rather you be an outcast, a freak, something at odds with the already. The best futures are anomalies. They are incalculable and volatile and unnerving.

Behind me, I heard a stream of urine hitting the marble.

"How'd you get out?" I asked.

"Harold's a friend of mine," said Pancake.

"Who's Harold?"

"The guard with the potbelly," he said, zipping up his pants. "I told him you were my son." Pancake surveyed the outside world, growing nervous and shifty, pacing back and forth. "Lana's probably worried sick about me."

I nodded in agreement.

"I'm gunna go steal a loaf of bread," he said.

We parted ways.

On the walk home, the future started happening. I spotted an auto repair shop on Atlantic, a run-down garage, and strolled inside. The owner's name was Louis, an older Hispanic man, who earned my trust immediately. Over the sound of mariachi tunes and power tools, I explained my situation to him: I had been arrested for drunk driving, my car was impounded, and I didn't have enough money to get the car back. If he loaned me money to get the car out, I would sell him the car for half of its value. He would be handed the keys upon my exiting the impound lot. Then he could do as he wished with the car. Selling it would earn him a significant profit. I provided him with my car's make and model and vehicle identification number. Still unsure if I was serious or not, he disappeared into his office and did some research on his computer, then reemerged.

"I can loan you the money," said Louis. "But you keep the car, sell it yourself, and you can just pay me back some interest. Not much, just a little extra cash, you know?"

"I'd rather you just buy it," I said. "I'll give it to you for almost nothing."

"No, no," he said. "I can pay for it. I just do not understand."

"It's a long story," I said.

Really it wasn't a long story. It was a rather short one: I needed the money now. Owing money to the IRS or a bank or a loan shark is fine, but owing money to the bartender is not. I had to pay back Gigi. A few thousand dollars would cover my debts to her, get a drink in my hands, and keep me afloat for the next few months. By then I'd have things figured out.

"We have a deal," said Louis.

I shook his hand, then we hopped in his rusted pickup truck and headed to the impound lot. On the way there, Louis lowered the radio and confided in me. "My son is gay," he said.

"How old is he?" I asked.

"Twenty."

"If I was gay, I would go on a date with him," I said.

Louis found this response very bizarre, as did I. He was so thrown off by it that he stopped confiding in me. A grueling silence ensued, a crippling vacuum. Louis tried to fill the void: He began whistling, he adjusted the mirrors, he scratched his neck. Slowly, though, his trust in me returned, his eyes flashing my way. Whatever ideas were serving time in his mind wanted out. They'd had enough. Words were coming. He needed an audience.

Louis must have been a very lonely man. And he obviously hadn't learned the most important skill of loneliness: talking to oneself. Don't worry, Louis. I will teach you. This is my craft. I study it. And here is the key: If you're going to be lonely, you must tell yourself things. Then you must respond to yourself. Become the others. It's a mild schizophrenia, really, madness on a leash. But if you master it, you will find success as a lonely man. You won't need anyone. You won't need me here in the passenger seat. You are the passenger. You are the bluebirds. You are the pretty girl at the bar. You are your dead grandparents. You are the lonely man who talks to ghosts.

"Antonio, that's my son's name," said Louis. "His boyfriend is William."

"It's good to have someone," I said.

"Yes," said Louis. "But I hear them, you know, in the bedroom."

"They live with you?"

Louis nodded. "Antonio's room is just above mine." He readjusted himself in his seat, bit the inside of his cheek, cracked his fingers. "The sounds are different, you know. They have to be, because of the way that they do it. Someone has to, you know, be on the bottom."

I nodded.

"They flip a coin," he continued. "The floors in my house, they are hardwood, so I can hear it. Sometimes the coin just drops right away, and that's it. Time to have fun. But sometimes it rolls, you know, it rolls around the floor, it rolls away from them. And they run after it, and they get very excited to see who will win."

"They're having a good time up there," I said.

"Yes," agreed Louis. "They are good boys." He cranked the radio up and played the drums on the steering wheel. "I will get carpets soon."

* * *

The stairs creaked beneath my feet.

The sound so reminded me of Nanna and Poppy that I deliberately slowed down, ascending the staircase like they had in their final years. I was Nanna, weak from the cancer, my joints failing, my youth a hazy thing before all this pain. Then I was Poppy. I supported Nanna up every step, her little hand in mine. For a few years, that's what happened on these stairs: Nanna never went up or down alone.

I offered to switch bedrooms with them, to move myself up to the second floor, but both of them refused. The stairs were not a burden to them. They were only something to be conquered together. They used to joke that, by the time they'd gotten down these stairs in the morning, it was time for a nap. And they would often do just that. Over steaming cups of coffee, they'd both read in the living room, Nanna on the couch with some Jane Austen or Toni Morrison, Poppy in his brown leather chair, lost in Fante or nodding to Kierkegaard. There was a serene duality about their morning ritual. Both were so immersed in books yet so together. There was the other world, the world of the page, and then there was the more important world: each other. Eventually they'd doze off together. Usually it was Poppy that fell asleep first, but that changed as Nanna got more sick.

The floral wallpaper at the top of the stairs was peeling, faded from the sunlight. As I made my way down the hallway, I stopped. I had to: They were in there. Why couldn't they just be in there, side by side in the bed, Poppy cracking jokes and Nanna unable to fall sleep because she can't stop laughing? I can hear them, like I used to. Poppy saying something, his words too faint to make out, then Nanna breaking into laughter. She tells him to shut up, to stop making her laugh. It's time to get some sleep. This would go on for a while, the fits of laughter, then the house would go quiet. It's been quiet ever since.

The door was open.

The room was a shell of its former self. It smelled of mildew and neglect. Anywhere that dust could settle, it had settled, on the floor and the bed, on Nanna's dresser and jewelry box, on the picture frames. The images of Nanna and Poppy and myself and friends and relatives, they were all murky, indistinct, the photographed figures trapped in the past, imprisoned behind a veil of dust.

Centered above the bed was a slanted crucifix.

I straightened it.

Poppy's painting of The Red Room, his favorite bar in Long Beach, had fallen off the wall. I returned it to its proper place. Along the windowsill were Nanna's many houseplants, all of them dead. There was no saving them. But among them was a lone cactus, undeterred by the drought and solitude, standing strong and defiant against the sun.

I am that cactus, I thought. I am alive and alone, jagged and dangerous to the touch, immune to the way of things. Things can die all around me, that's fine. Go ahead and die. I will endure.

I turned to the bookshelf. It spanned the entire northern wall of the bedroom. I built it with my bare hands, Poppy told me. Nanna chimed in with the real story: This was the third of Poppy's bookshelves. The previous two had collapsed. Poppy defended his honor, claiming the collapses were only because of the weight, because the two of them had collected so many books, and not because his building methods were unsound. Maybe you should read some books on woodworking, Nanna remarked. Nietzsche doesn't teach carpentry, does he? No, replied Poppy. He killed Joseph's son. Friedrich didn't get along too well with the carpenters.

Thousands of books.

Vonnegut, Bukowski, Dazai, Dostoevsky, Austen, Toni Morrison. Every philosophy book ever written, from Heraclitus to Ayn Rand. There was Orwell on the top shelf, John Fante down on the bottom. Bandini would appreciate being down there in the gutter, Poppy told me. There was Freud and Jung, Joseph Campbell and Robert Pirsig. There was Frank Herbert, Balzac, Hesse, Rimbaud, Tolstoy, Dawkins, Steinbeck, Goethe. There were too many titles to count, so many worlds to explore, so much to learn and unlearn.

For a fleeting moment, there was nostalgia. Many of these books, whichever ones Nanna and Poppy had put into my hands, I had read. But I had given up on reading. I had given up on it like I had given up on everything else. Was there anything I hadn't given up on?

Nanna and Poppy are over there, lounging on the bed. They're both wondering the same things I've been wondering: What happened to you? What happened to that book you wanted to write? I thought about escaping to another room, but I couldn't turn my back on them. What do you stand for? I don't know. What do you do? Nothing. I do nothing, but I do it well. What will they say about you when you die? I'm still young. There is plenty of time. Come to think of it, this, right here, is one of my talents. Right or wrong, I can rationalize my position. My two great skills: drinking rum and winning arguments against the deceased.

There was no rum in the house, so I sat down on the bed, dust circling, and told myself things like this:

I am a bluebird.

To strive is to be let down by the hollow results of striving.

To care is to end up like those plants, dead and brown and gone for good.

I haven't given up.

I have only grown wise to the fact that nothing is worth it.

I am what I have to be, Ruthless like The Now.

But these were lies. I knew they were lies, even before I thought them. And they weren't your average lies either. They were big ones. Lies this good, the ones of the foundational variety, always give birth to more lies. They are so heavy that they need immediate support. So I told myself another lie, one I'd learned from a saint: Drinks are needed.

* * *

I walk quietly up the front porch. Through the window, I see that the dining room light is on. I must have left it on before going out. I need to drink less. That's what I'll do, yeah. I need to lay off the beers.

Reaching to open the door, I hear him. I hear Poppy. I hear the sobs. And I know. So I stop for a moment, frozen. I am too drunk for this moment. I consider turning around, finding a park bench to cry on. Or I could sleep it off on the beach and face this in the morning.

But I don't want him to be alone.

"She's gone," says Poppy as I enter the dining room.

I don't know what to say, so I take a seat across from him. He knows how I feel. Words aren't necessary. They will be insufficient.

He disappears into the kitchen. I hear ice clink into a glass. I realize, now, that the glass already on the table isn't water. Poppy returns with my glass and a bottle of vodka.

"Drinks are needed," he says.

I nod.

"What do we do now?" he asks no one in particular.

He makes his vodka disappear, the way he used to. I do away with mine too. Poppy pours us both another, then stares at the dining room table. He sees her face in it, in everything.

"What a lady she was," says Poppy.

"The best," I say.

"The very best," he says.

He holds out his glass. I tap mine on his. The clink is exactly the right pitch. It is celestial, important. It resounds through the first floor. Sometimes the glasses don't quite play the right music. This time they did. They know this means something.

"She's up there in heaven causing quite a stir," says Poppy. "The Apostles are going to be chasing after her. She'll have the priests questioning their celibacy."

I chuckle.

"Married to God or married to Nanna?" he says.

"It's not even a question," I say.

"You know, I never did understand prayer," he says. "On the one hand, God knows everything. On the other, we're supposed to talk to him. But what is there to say to the man who knows everything? What could possibly be said?" He loses himself in thought for a moment. "Parts of the Bible are genius, but a lot of it's just bad writing. If the man's omniscient, the best option is just to leave the poor guy alone. Imagine a gang of people calling you every day to tell you things you already knew. Talk about annoying."

"Yeah," I say. "And on top of that, they're all looking for favors."

Poppy chuckles.

I do too.

"It's gotta be a boring life for the Lord," continues Poppy. "You have all the answers. Now what? How do you spend your time? What do you do with your days? Do you—"

He breaks off into contemplation.

Down goes his drink.

"I'll tell you what you do," says Poppy. "If God's smart, he'll ask Nanna on a date. That'll change things. Ten minutes in and he'll realize he doesn't have all the fucking answers. She'll make that clear. His whole metaphysical outlook will go to shit. She'll poke a few holes in his ego, have him questioning himself. Knock the good Lord down to earth a bit. By the time dessert comes out, he won't be so damn sure of himself."

"God, the atheist," I say.

"Good book title for you when the time comes," says Poppy with a grin.

We laugh at God, but the laughter only holds up the defenses for so long.

Eventually the tears come.

Lots of them.

We give moisture to the dead, jokes Poppy.

There are more drinks.

Then more.

I know he won't live much longer.

BEER

Gigi, the time has come to heed your advice. It is no doubt good advice, and that's why I had to ignore it: It hit too close to home. So I had to let it sit and ferment for a while. I had to distill it, to decouple it from you, so that I could feel as though the idea was my own. Nonetheless, here we are. Today I am saying goodbye to my precious rum. My dearest Gigi, I will take a beer. Please do keep them coming....

Chapter 19

*...for it, nothing would be uncertain and the future, as the past,
would be present to its eyes.*
—Pierre-Simon Laplace

Comfort came to me as I neared the door.

There was the scent of popcorn and mildew. There was the breaking of a glass. There was a thin fog of cigarette smoke drifting out onto the sidewalk. As I got close enough, there was Mr. John's radio, the faint classical music. It might have been Bach, it might have been Mozart, it didn't matter. It was something to believe in.

"He comes back," said Mr. John.

I nodded.

"We must go away sometimes," he said.

I agreed.

Mr. John asked if I had something to smoke for him, then, lighting up the cigarette, he stared at me and smiled, prodding with his soft gaze. If I had to put words to it, he was saying something like: *You took a trip within, good boy. Did you find anything worthwhile?*

Well, Mr. John, I haven't exactly cured myself. But introspection has happened. And that's often the best one can do: Take a look inside and wait. The answers don't come right away, nor do they come in the form of words. They arrive first as feelings, planted seeds, opaque murmurs. If properly watered and attended to, they can sprout into words. Then, finally, if fostered to maturity, these feelings-turned-words can become convictions. But it's quite a process, Mr. John. We don't get to choose what the mind says. It takes time and effort to sculpt an identity out of the endless flow of nonsense generated by the brain. If anyone can understand and appreciate a slow-moving metamorphosis, it's you, Mr. John. Whatever glass Pancake just shattered inside, you'll surely sweep into a pile beneath the pool table and place a coaster atop it. The actual cleanup will take place sometime in the next two months. You know it as well as I do: Good things take time.

Into the bar I went.

I knew it would take a while to catch up with everyone. The less your friends are doing with their lives, the more there is to catch up about. On the road to nowhere, every small victory must be celebrated, for there are no big ones.

Lana opened up by smacking me in the face and demanding that I find her shoe. I promised I would. Then she went on for twenty minutes about how she had found a new spot for the tent, ten yards from its former spot. The purpose of the relocation was to outsmart the police via technicality. When the blueys returned, Lana and Pancake would insist that they did indeed relocate. It would hold up in court, she insisted.

Gigi detailed some of Pancake's recent indiscretions. He had showed up a few days prior with a full honey-glazed ham, urinated on the ham in the alley, regretted doing it, and requested that Gigi rinse the ham with the soda hose. Then he ate some of the ham, he passed out on top of the pool table, etc.

Fresh off a meth blast, Pancake bulldozed in from the alley to tell his side of things. He confirmed most of the tale but clarified a few key details. He did not regret urinating on the ham. This was hearsay. Instead, he had chosen to urinate on the ham to prove to Edgar that the ham was so good that it would retain its deliciousness despite being urinated on. This was true, Pancake assured us, for the ham remained delicious. Edgar corroborated this story. Apparently half of the urine-ham was still stored in the kitchen freezer, and Pancake planned to enjoy it *when the time felt right.*

The last snippet of news was that Penny had learned a new word. It's another way to say *smart*, she told me. Then she forced me to guess the word as she smoked a cigarette and bottle-fed her baby nephew with the same hand. The other hand needed to be free to navigate the jukebox. I rattled off five or six guesses with no luck. Grinning with pride, she informed me that the word was *erudite.* She'd heard it on a television show and looked it up on the internet. She'd even written it down. But she expressed concern as to why there were multiple ways to say the same thing. The choices disoriented her.

I insisted that more words meant more freedom of expression. She disagreed, arguing that everyone plays favorites anyhow, as if she had to pick either smart or erudite to keep in her vocabulary arsenal. After some deliberation, she put out her cigarette and decided that she would not be using erudite moving forward. I supported this. I wasn't a fan of erudite. There are some words that, by their very pronunciation, ooze pretentiousness. I mentioned this to Penny, using the word *pontificate* as an example. To even use the word pontificate is to pontificate, I said. Penny had not a clue what I meant, and I realized that I had let some of my own pretentiousness slip out. She did what was correct and offered to put on some Frankie Miller if I left her alone and never said that word again. A deal was reached.

Finally, I was up to speed.

There's an unease that comes with being away from the debauchery. In the world of drinks, it's not so much a fear of missing out on things, because every memory in this bar is so hazy that the details are just placeholders. In the long run, no one remembers who was there on a specific night and who was not. In two months, the urine-ham story might very well involve me. Don't you remember? I was here. I was most certainly here, my friends. I urinated on the ham too. It was so fun. I have never missed a night in this place. My picture will be up on that wall someday with the legends. I was born in here, and I will die in here.

What truly bothered me about being away from this place was the disrespect, the hubris it takes to think I have something better to do than sit in a stool and drink and laugh at the billions of people who aren't lucky enough to be us.

"This time I really thought you'd done away with yourself," said Gigi. "Like seriously, I was pretty sure I'd never see you again."

"I'm just finalizing the suicide note," I said, holding an invisible gun to my head and pulling the trigger. "How long do you think it would take Mr. John to clean up the mess?"

"A thousand miles," said Gigi.

We laughed.

"You wouldn't shoot yourself though," said Gigi. "That's too easy. You'd cook up some strange way to do it. You'd stab yourself in the back and make it look like a homicide. Or hang yourself right out here in the back alley with a note for the garbage men to *handle with care* or something like that."

"Both of those are viable options," I said.

"I'm here for you," said Gigi.

As she poured me another, I plucked three crisp hundreds from my wad of cash and set them down on the bar. "I do not come empty-handed."

"Wow," said Gigi. "Did you whore yourself out?"

"I sold my car."

"That won't solve things."

"I'm selling the house too."

"That won't solve things either."

"Thanks for the support," I said.

"You don't want people supporting you," she said. "That means you need it." She poured herself a shot of whiskey and did away with it.

"So you assumed I killed myself," I said. "And yet you didn't come check on me? No knock on the door? No phone call? Nothing?"

"You wouldn't have answered. You're dead."

"You could have called the coroner."

"I have a job," she said.

* * *

Someone had ordered Chinese food.

I was playing pool against a black woman named Chalize, a DMV employee who stops in every few weeks, but I couldn't focus on the game. Over on the bar was a take-out container piled high with fried rice and noodles and some kind of overcooked chicken. The food itself looked very low-quality, but its fragrance was enchanting. It overwhelmed the bar. There's something about the smell of cheap, Americanized Chinese food, the salt and the spices and the cholesterol. This specific blend of ingredients pings some primal region of the brain. When Chinese food is in the area, it's nearly impossible to have other goals. It feels like lust, like sexual desire.

"If someone doesn't get to work on that plate," said Chalize. "I will have to handle it."

"It has to be done," I agreed.

"Oh, you guys go ahead," said Penny. "I'm not hungry."

"Seriously?" asked Chalize.

"Yeah," said Penny. "I was going to eat it, but my stomach is acting up." She gulped some Budweiser and passed the baby off to Gigi, then disappeared into the bathroom.

Chalize put her arm around me and said, "You and me, baby, we split this thing fifty-fifty. Does that sound fair?"

I nodded.

She grabbed a popcorn tray and hustled over to the Chinese food. Her mind spinning with ideas, she again returned to the popcorn trays, grabbed a second tray, then raced over to the kitchen doorway. "You got a scale back there?" she asked Edgar.

"No," said Edgar. "The weight, I do it with my eyes."

"We don't need to weigh it," I said. "It doesn't have to be exact. You can have more than me."

"You sure?" asked Chalize, eyeing up the Chinese food. "The chicken will be easy. We can just count the pieces, split it down the middle. It's the rice and noodles, they're gunna be tricky. The math won't hold up. It's—"

"Yea, it's fine," I said. "You can have the bigger half."

Chalize hugged me then divided up the Chinese food. The two of us sat in silence at the bar and ate for a few minutes, devouring everything on our plates. Then it was over. Was it worth it? Sure, we had followed our hearts, but had it led us to happiness? No. It brought about only regret, the sound of the devil's laughter. Chalize got up and left the bar without saying a word. It felt like a one-night stand.

Ten minutes later, Mr. John came wandering into the bar looking for his Chinese food. Apparently the delivery man had walked right by him while he was sleeping.

"You told us it was yours," I said to Penny.

"I never said that," she replied.

"Well, you didn't say it wasn't yours."

"Well, I knew you wanted to eat it," she said, smiling at me.

I could tell now that Penny was uncharacteristically drunk, her grin crooked, her eyes glossy. She was incessantly burping, her whole body convulsing as she did so. She set the baby down on top of the bar, face-up, and pulled out her little diabetes kit. With drunken grace, she pricked her finger and tested her blood glucose levels. "Time to fix it," she muttered to herself. Then she jabbed an insulin needle into her belly. Once the shot was administered, she leaned back in her stool, ran her hands through her hair, and said, "What a life we have here."

She heard me chuckling at her.

"Come over here," she said. "Let's test your levels, sweet pea."

I hopped down a few barstools, settling in beside Penny. She pricked my finger and gathered some blood. After a moment of calculation, the machine beeped. "Holy cow," said Penny.

"Is it bad?" I asked.

"Your blood sugar is through the roof," she exclaimed with excitement.

"Too much rum," Gigi chimed in.

"You'll be Type 2 before you know it," said Penny with a supporting pat on my thigh. "There's no two ways about it." Then, without even warning me, she stabbed a needle into the outside of my arm, pumping some insulin into me.

"Is this safe?" I asked.

"It's a lifestyle," said Penny, repacking her diabetes kit and storing it away. She then scooped up the baby and kissed his forehead, rocking him back and forth in her arms, singing something into his ear.

Gigi and I shared a knowing glance. Both of us recognized Penny's level of inebriation. Usually she could drink and drink and drink and remain the same. Tonight, she was different. She was content, it seemed. She couldn't stop smiling. And she'd only scratched one or two scratch-offs.

"You know, I really love you guys," said Penny. "You guys are the best."

"We love you too, Penny-girl," said Gigi.

I nodded.

"There's just no better place than this," continued Penny. "You can go anywhere in this city, anywhere in the whole country, and it's not like this. I've been to Arizona, and I went to San Diego once. But there was nowhere special like this. I looked, and there just wasn't. Other places are different. But us, we have something good here. There's all of us, together like this. We have each other here, at least. We have me, we have you," she said, touching my shoulder. "We have Edgar, we have Mr. John."

Pancake strolled in from the back alley.

"We have Pancake," said Penny. "Give it up for Pancake." Pancake clapped for himself and started barehanding popcorn out of the machine.

"And we have Gigi," said Penny with tears in her eyes. "We love you, Gigi. We love you to the moon and back. We really, really love you, Gigi."

"And I love you too, Penny," responded Gigi, gifting her a tequila shot.

Tears started streaming down Penny's face. Gigi walked around the bar and hugged her. Penny said it again: "What a life we have here."

Seizing the opportunity, Pancake stole her tequila shot.

I thought about saying something to Penny, something supportive, but no words assembled themselves. Part of me considered her declaration ridiculous, a drunken statement that was so overtly obvious that it wasn't worthy of being voiced in the first place. Of course we love it here, Penny. That's why we're here, why we're always here. But another part of me felt inhuman. I was distant and ungrateful. Why couldn't I be like Penny? Why couldn't I, for once in my life, say such things?

Tell them you love them, you fool.

Tell them you would be dead without them.

Tell them you've dreamed of your funeral.

And they weren't there.

Tell them how it devastated you.

Tell them everything.

FREE WILL

With just one short life to live, we humans get to die off before accepting that free will does not exist. Nothing about the mechanics of the universe points in the direction of free will. And, beyond pure numbers, some among us always have a suspicion, a hunch, a feeling that we are, as the man beneath the floorboards feared, only piano keys being played by the universe. Certain moments in my life seem too fateful to be a product of my own volition. Did I really have a choice? No, I don't think I did. My thoughts have always just sprouted out of thin air. I am an antenna at best. But a human life simply doesn't last long enough for this idea to fully set in, to grow roots and become a fact. To stop believing in God or Santa Claus takes ten or fifteen years. To stop believing in free will, though, takes longer than a lifetime. One hundred years is not enough time to erode human pride, to adequately convince one that he is not the author of his own life. Nature has indeed designed the perfect lifespan, for our bodily death always precedes the death of the ego. Thus, we humans are blessed to arrive at the grave only suspecting what, if we were given a thousand years to live, we would have inevitably come to know: Life is a book to be read, not a story to be written. We are taken on a ride, historians masquerading as kings....

Chapter 20

Be silent and listen: have you recognized your madness and do you admit it?
—Carl Jung

We were getting some fresh air out back. Edgar had the kitchen door propped open with his blue two-by-four, the fragrance of frying chicken wings leaking into the alley.

"I think when we die, we go back to the beginning," said Edgar.

"We start life over?" I asked.

"Yes, we do it again."

"The eternal return!" screamed Pancake.

"So we just keep restarting life?" I asked. "Infinite times?"

Edgar shook his head and, with supreme confidence, held up three fingers.

"We live three times," I inferred.

He nodded stoically, then said, "Maybe four or five."

"I like that," I said. "We get a few cracks at it, but we don't overdo it."

A fly landed on the rim of my drink, bringing the dialogue to a halt.

"Shhh," whispered Pancake. I handed him the glass. He lifted it slowly to his face, the fly nearly touching his eyeball. "Worry not, Señor Fly. Your death is only the beginning."

"Unless it's his fifth death," I said.

"Then he is dead," said Edgar.

Pancake took my glass over to the Beauty to have some private time with the fly. He set the drink gently on the back bumper and slid a milk crate over to take a seat beside it.

"It wouldn't make sense if we were born an infinite number of times," I said.

"Yes," said Edgar. "It is too much."

"If you lived a good life over and over again, that would get boring. So you'd want to throw a bad life in there to make things interesting again. Be a saint for three lives, then go on a killing spree the fourth. That's the way we are. We want something new. Even the fun gets boring."

Edgar nodded thoughtfully, shutting his eyes, imagining quasi-eternal life.

"But even if you did that," I continued. "If you intentionally mixed up the kind of lives you were living, a pattern would eventually develop. You might not know it right away, but over time you'd realize that you'd fallen into a routine. It's human nature. Ten good lives, one bad one, six bad, one good, then repeat—something like that. It's almost like the longer cycles of the economy. If you only look at the short term, you can be fooled into thinking it's chaos. But the big picture always tells the real story. We're as predictable as the day is long. We have very little control."

I wanted to go further. I wanted to grab Edgar by the face and ask him: Don't you feel it too, Papi? The universe has us by the balls. The instant the Big Bang banged, we were destined to end up here in this alley, the moon hovering between those telephone poles. We're pool balls off the break. We've never had a choice. This wagon has no reins. As we age, we try to convince ourselves that we've got it figured out, but we don't. We are only babies with an expanded vocabulary. We don't get better at making decisions. We only get better at explaining past ones. We become excellent publicists for the former versions of ourselves. Yes, the brightest among us can get the news out quickly, but we are never ahead of the curve. We're always a precious moment behind The Ruthless Now. I tried to explain this same thing to a seagull once, but this rendition came out more smoothly. I'm still refining it, working out the details.

Edgar's eyes slowly opened. Something about my message hit home with him. He pressed his hand to my chest, feeling for my heartbeat. "I have something for you," he said, disappearing into the kitchen. Edgar kept an entire closet of belongings behind the industrial refrigerator, everything from family heirlooms to neglected tax documents in a disorganized heap. I heard him digging through his stash, filtering through his life, searching for whatever item my existential rant had jostled loose from his memory.

He returned with a bottle of tequila.

"The fly," he said. "He has stolen your drink."

"Live fast, die middle-aged," I said, swigging the bottle.

"Yes, I know your plan," said Edgar. "Life fast, die in the middle."

Pancake parted ways with the fly and rejoined us over the bottle. It was decided that fate had done its job: It had brought the three of us here to this alley. It was now our job to finish all the tequila, eat two dozen chicken wings, and see where the evening took us. We owed it to each other. You only live between three and five times.

* * *

Something is not right.

Tequila does not sit well with me.

Did I leave the house unlocked?

I don't think so.

Is today Nanna's birthday? No.

Poppy's? No.

...life must be understood backwards.

There it is.

I like that one.

But I don't like this feeling. It's the same feeling I had on the night Poppy died. Disquiet in a place of comfort. Something is amiss. It's easier to have a thousand problems staring you in the face than to endure a single obscure worry. The silence, the silence, the silence.

That's it: silence.

There is no dripping.

What has happened to the Sacred Sink?

Where is the usual magic?

Say it for me.

Drip, drip, drip.

When are you going to let me catch up?

Drip, drip, drip.

Pancake screams. Someone probably harmed a fly.

Gigi shouts, then Lana, then Penny.

It's all getting louder.

I hurry out of the bathroom.

"You didn't want any popcorn?!" screams Pancake, a broken-off pool stick in his hand.

Gigi holds him back from Joseph A, standing very calmly beside the bar. "Pancake, stop it, okay?!" says Gigi. "He's not here to cause trouble!"

"He's just back to stare at the popcorn machine again!" thunders Pancake.

"Fuck this guy," I say, stepping up beside Pancake.

"You stay outta this," says Gigi.

"He's a fuckin' lifeguard!" yells Pancake. "Here to save us all!" He hurls a can of beans at Joseph A, but it misses, breaking one of the window panels on the front door. This wakes up Mr. John, asleep in his chair by the door. He does nothing.

Pancake shoves Gigi out of the way. I try to catch her before she goes to the ground, but we both end up falling.

"The time is now!" screams Pancake.

"Rain, Sarge!" he sings in support. "Rain, rain, rain!"

Pancake digs his feet into the floor like a bull preparing to charge, then storms forward at full speed. Joseph A prepares to fight, but upon seeing Pancake's reckless approach, opts to simply move out of the way, allowing Pancake's own inertia to send him headfirst into the claw machine. He is immediately out cold, his body limp. Even though he's unconscious, you can tell he's supremely fucked up by the way his body is impossibly contorted, his elbow bending the wrong way. He's either double jointed or blacked out, and I've never heard Pancake boast about his flexibility.

His head must have smashed into the START button because the claw machine's happy little jingle comes on. Someone must have forgotten to play a turn. The metal claw lifts into position.

Joseph A pulls up his sleeves, ready to fight. Every inch of his arms are covered in tattoos. "I'll have to put in a little more effort with you," he says. "But it'll be the same deal. I'll lay you right down next to your friend here while we wait for the cops."

"Go fuck yourself," I say.

"Will that be all?" he asks.

I didn't think it was possible to be nervous after this many drinks, but I was. My legs shook at the knees. Nothing was supposed to matter, but this night was trying to. Standing there frozen, I imagined myself stepping forward, fighting Joseph A, getting knocked out with a single punch, honoring my strong tradition of losing fights. Another black eye for the collection. Down goes the bluebird once again.

I started laughing at myself.

"Is something funny?" asked Joseph A.

"Not at all," I said.

The timer ran out on the claw machine. The claw dropped down and clamped shut on Camilla's head, perfectly grabbing her by the neck. It was hilarious that the machine, without anyone operating the claw, had done a better job than any of us ever had.

Up went the claw, briefly lifting Camilla out of captivity, but she slipped away and fell back into her place among the stuffed animals. I glanced at everyone, at Gigi and Penny and Lana. We all saw it: Among the stuffed animals, hiding underneath Camilla, was Lana's left shoe.

It always turns up.

* * *

Joseph A was out in the back alley.

"Go back there and talk to him," said Gigi.

"About what?" I asked. "I just almost fought the guy."

"Trust me. You two will get along."

"You know him?"

She nodded. "Go," she said with sincerity.

I downed my drink and walked out back. Joseph A was leaning on the back bumper of the Beauty, smoking a cigarette. I arrived beside him and lit one up for myself.

"You can smoke inside, you know," I said.

He nodded.

"Grandfathered in kind of thing," I explained. "This place has been here since the 60s, before they made it illegal to smoke in bars."

"1967," he said. "Hasn't changed much since."

"You used to come here?" I asked.

"Every day," he said. "I own the place."

A stale silence enveloped us. I heard the buzzing of the electrical wires, the crackling of my cigarette, the dry palm leaves rustling in the wind.

"Fuck," I said.

"Don't worry about it," he said.

"So you're Hugh?"

"Frank," he said. "My dad was Hugh."

"Why the Two?"

"He used to order two drinks at a time," said Frank. "One drink is lonely, that's what he used to say."

"I like that," I said, studying him in the moonlight. Up close, I could see the details of his face. He had a small scar above his left eye, deep wrinkles across his cheeks. There was pain, and it was familiar. "One of those pictures is you, isn't it? Behind the bar."

He nodded.

"Did you fix the sink?" I asked.

"I did," he said. "I'm trying to fix the place up just enough to keep it fucked. Get a new popcorn machine, replace the carpet, nothing too crazy."

"That's how you know Gigi?" I asked. "You're co-owners."

"I was married to her," he said. "Now she's married to this place."

He was smoking his cigarette very slowly, savoring it. He inhaled, exhaled, then let the smoke explore before continuing: "That's what my current wife doesn't understand. She doesn't get it, you know. She's like most people. She walks in here and sees nothing but a shithole. She keeps begging me to sell the place and move on, but Gigi's not having it, which is perfect because I don't wanna sell it either, so I can just blame Gigi as if she's the problem."

"It's a great place," I said.

He nodded, still enjoying that cigarette.

"I think I saw your wife in here once," I said.

"Yeah," said Frank. "She came by to give Gigi some paperwork, information about the real estate market, trying to make her case."

"Gigi threw 'em in the trash," I told him.

"Sounds about right."

"You quit drinking?" I asked.

"Had no choice," said Frank. "They don't have the good kind of bars in prison."

I apologized about the animosity. Frank wasn't offended in the slightest. He admitted that he did in fact stick around that first night to watch us. But it wasn't judgment. It was nostalgia. We reminded him of the good old days.

Again, I couldn't help but laugh at myself.

"What's funny?" asked Frank.

"Just the whole scenario," I said.

"What about it?"

"I don't know," I said. "How we thought we hated you and yet you turn out to be the owner of the bar. It's like, maybe the real level of animosity in the world is far lower than we assume, because the animosity itself is built on meaningless foundations. It's pure speculation. And then the person you hate hates you back, but only because you hated them first. One person cooks up enmity out of thin air, based on nonsense, and suddenly you have a conflict. Right there we can assume that a majority of the world's hatred is false. Who was actually the first person to hate? For all we know, all of our hatred may go back to the Garden of Eden. Adam and Eve probably had one meaningless marital fight, Cain and Abel had to pick sides, and we know how that one ended. We've been at war ever since."

"This is what I deal with every day," said Gigi, silhouetted in the doorway.

"I like this guy," said Frank.

"He's not bad," said Gigi.

"I take it you're the one scribbling those quotes all over the bathroom," said Frank.

"Sorry about that," I said.

"He's a writer," said Gigi.

"Are you?" asked Frank.

"A writer that doesn't write," she clarified.

"I'm planning," I said.

"That's good," said Frank. "I'm planning on opening up an Italian restaurant."

"Where?" I asked. "Around here?"

"He's been planning it since the 80s," said Gigi.

The two shared a laugh.

He went on to explain that his half-baked Italian restaurant dream was made impossible once he got caught up in the cocaine scene. One thing led to another, and the bar was going under, so he got desperate. He and a friend robbed three pharmacies and were charged with armed robbery. He did twelve years, four in North Kern, eight in San Quentin. He'd gotten out a year and a half ago. The money from those robberies, however, did keep the bar afloat. Gigi had made sure of it.

Eventually Pancake stumbled outside and had no recollection of the confrontation. I introduced him to Frank and explained the situation.

Pancake was dumbfounded and ashamed. He argued with himself about how to right his wrong, choosing to go inside and gift Frank an enormous tray of popcorn lathered in the Mixture. Frank accepted graciously. As it turned out, Frank's best friend and Pancake were second cousins. The two hugged it out, then Frank grabbed a bag of ice from inside and handed it to Pancake to deal with the swelling on his forehead.

Closing time came around.

But we kept drinking in the alley.

It was one of those nights that was tough to walk away from. Gigi brought out a few cases of beer. She refused to serve me any more rum, so I switched over to beers. You need to give up the rum, she told me yet again. Yes, I will, Gigi. One day I will, I promise you. Edgar cooked up a chicken wing feast. We wished Penny and the baby farewell. It was past his bedtime. She thought about laying him down to rest in the Beauty, but Mr. John had already come out back and claimed that spot. He was sleeping peacefully, with a gentle snore, his feet dangling out the trunk.

Frank and Gigi told us old Hugh Two stories. It was a popular biker hangout for many decades. The Beauty was actually Frank's car, the same one he and his best friend had used in the robbery. They'd parked it back here to hide it, and it hadn't moved in the many years since. We told Frank that we use it for naps, sexual escapades, and drugs. He was glad to hear it was serving the cause.

Before we knew it, the sun started to rise. This prompted a clean-up effort. All of us spread out over the alley, tossing away trash and sweeping up broken bottles. Edgar dumped the used kitchen grease onto the pavement, and Gigi hosed it away, the oils reflecting the early morning glow.

I was picking up cigarette butts around the dumpster when I heard him: a bluebird. He was swooping through a nearby backyard, calling out to me with his unmistakable shrieks.

There you are, my friend.

Your blood is my blood.

Were you here the whole time, enjoying the party with us?

What a night this was, the turn of events.

Yes, I know, the humans are not ideal.

I let out a squawk.

"Bluebird," I announced to the humans.

"That's a western scrub jay, actually," said Frank.

"Is it?" I asked.

He nodded. "I've had too much time on my hands over the years. I know every bird call there is." Frank let out his imitation scrub jay call. It was spot-on, a perfect match. "Scrubs jays are smart bastards, some of the most intelligent birds on the planet. But they're ruthless creatures. They'll steal from other birds, steal from each other, you name it. Apparently if one of them dies, though, they have a fucking bird funeral. They all get together and scream away over the dead body."

The scrub jay let out a final squawk as it flew away, disappearing over Hugh Two.

I let out another shriek.

Frank followed suit.

Gigi and Edgar gave it their best shot.

Pancake squawked to the sky, then responded to himself with another.

Mr. John opened his eyes and smiled, then went back to sleep.

LAUGHTER

Laughter is the laundering of despair, no different than drinking. And, conveniently, the laughing man and the drinking man can usually acquire their fix in the same places, a two-for-one deal. I myself purchase them at the corner store. I shell out for them in creaky bars. I load up at happy hours. I bargain for them during every fucked up little moment the world throws at me. But I have mostly bought them in solitude, to deal with the sadness, to carry me through long periods of existing with myself. Crack a joke or crack a bottle. They're best in combination. But the laughs and the drinks, they add up. When a night on the town becomes a life on the town, the tab inevitably runs too high, beyond what you can afford. And you realize you've been paying for it with your life....

Chapter 21

It is perfectly true, as the philosophers say, that life must be understood backwards.
But they forget the other proposition, that it must be lived forwards.
—Søren Kierkegaard

There were flies trapped in the rum.

Around noon, I was boxing up some things when I noticed them, those flies, hundreds and hundreds of them. They were stuck to the dining room table, fossilized in the rum veneer. Did these flies die all at once, a kind of genocide? Or had they been steadily dying, month by month, day by day? I didn't know. But they were dead, all of them. They had been drawn in by the sweet nectar and paid the highest price.

I wiped down the table.

Once it was clean, I took a seat and ran my hand along the surface. I no longer like this table, I thought. I don't like it one bit. My first inclination was to go to Port Liquor, buy a bottle of rum, and pour it over the table. It has lost its shine. And I really did consider doing this. But before I could take off out the front door, I caught myself. To pour rum over the dining room table, that is preposterous.

But is it?

Yes.

No, no, it's not.

I made my way over to the window. The glass itself was caked in dust, so much so that I could barely see out. There was a world out there, that I knew.

There were the plants and the animals and the humans. But from in here, none of it meant much. I should wipe down this window, I thought. I should wipe down all of the windows. No one is going to buy a house if the windows are this dirty. It's depressing. A house needs proper sunlight.

Where are you, my friends?

I have a confession to make.

I laughed. Because that's what a human would do. Talking to birds again, are we? Yes. Yes, I am. Allow me this, just one last time.

Listen, my friends.

As it turns out, I am not a bluebird.

But it's fine.

Neither are you.

None of us are bluebirds.

We are blue birds.

Do you understand?

I continued packing up Nanna and Poppy's things, neatly stacking old picture frames and cookbooks into boxes. Then I moved into the kitchen. I cleared out the fridge. I tossed away every item in the pantry. I cleaned the microwave, scraping away the charred remnants of lasagna, layer by layer. Somewhere in this house, I told myself, I will find Nanna's lasagna recipe, and I will prepare one last meal here. I will cook it the proper way. I will sit at the dining room table and eat alone. But I will not be alone. It will be me and Nanna and Poppy. And at the head of the table will be God, the atheist. He will laugh with us about how he used to believe in himself, that fool. I hope you like lasagna, God, otherwise you can see yourself out. You're not that important. The more delicate items, the china and the various glassware, would need to be bubble-wrapped before being packed away. That's the way Nanna would have done it. She wouldn't want them breaking. But that was a job for a different day.

I went to sleep.

* * *

I didn't make it to Hugh Two until later in the night.

Mr. John and I exchanged shoulder massages on my way in. I wanted to smoke a cigarette with him, but there was only one left in the pack.

"Something to smoke for you," I said, offering it to him.

"Something to smoke for we," he said.

We passed the cigarette back and forth for a few minutes. No words were spoken, but the silence itself was a kind of dialogue. Every time Mr. John handed me the cigarette, he looked me in the eyes and nodded as if he felt something different about me. Was there a difference? Another day was lined up before me. I wanted to kick this hangover. I wanted to sit there in my usual barstool and think, to find some things to laugh about, to let the world come to me over a drink. But I wanted so much more than that too.

"The end is for you," said Mr. John, gifting me the last of the dying cigarette. He plopped down in his metal folding chair, closed his eyes, and within seconds was snoring gently.

I made my way to the bar.

"I heard it was a late one in the back alley," said Penny.

"Very late," I said.

"You look like a man in need of Frankie," said Penny.

I nodded. On came Frankie Miller's soothing raspiness, narrating my life from the jukebox. Penny began scratching a scratch-off ticket. She would surely lose. Then she would lose again. But maybe she would hit it big again one of these days. Some people do win. That crowd just doesn't tend to come in here very often.

Pancake begged me to play pool, but I told him I needed some time to get my feet under me. Lana played with him instead. I complimented her on having two shoes on. She threatened to hurt me, then rescinded when I offered to buy her and Pancake drinks.

Gigi came out from the kitchen with a fresh batch of limes to cut. Spotting me, she remembered something. "I've gotta run to my car," she said, setting down the limes and leaving out the front door.

While she was gone, I noticed everyone eyeing me.

Penny grinned a devious grin.

Pancake exchanged whispers with himself.

Lana floated over to the kitchen door to alert Edgar.

Gigi returned with a black and white marble notebook, the kind elementary school students use. She rounded the bar, grabbing a pen from beside the cash register, then dropped the notebook in front of me.

"If you want a drink," she said. "You've gotta write something down."

"What?"

"Frank's orders," she said.

"Stop fucking around," I said.

"Look, it doesn't matter to me," she said. "It's his rule."

"I'm struggling here, Gigi."

"I can see that," she said. "So just write something: the Pledge of Allegiance, the Our Father, a nice suicide note, whatever you want. But if you wanna be served, you'll have to write something down first. Then you can have all the drinks you want."

"One drink would really help get the juices flowing," I said.

She shook her head.

"A suicide note it is," I said, heading off to the bathroom.

I took a seat on the toilet.

The bathroom was eerie without the broken sink. I wanted to do the right thing and fix it, loosen up the faucet, get it dripping again. But maybe Frank is right, I thought. Some small improvements wouldn't kill anyone. Hopefully in time the cycle would repeat itself—the Sacred Sink would fall into disrepair and start dripping again. The chicken and the egg.

In the meantime, I had to use my imagination.

Drip, drip, drip.

There it is.

Drip, drip, drip.

A pacemaker for the heartless.

What a life we have here.

When I walked out of the bathroom a few minutes later, as I had expected, everyone was gathered around the bar waiting for me, including three strangers, respectable suburban people I'd never seen before.

Penny muted the jukebox.

Pancake snatched the notebook from my hand and climbed atop the bar:

<u>HUGH TWO</u>

I love this bar. I love the torn carpets. I love the shattered mirrors. I love the gaping holes in the ceiling. I love the warped bartop, the drinks gathering in its valleys like lakes. I love the popcorn machine, the way it hisses. I love the aroma of stale beer and overcooked buffalo wings and cigarettes. I love the pool table, that beautiful 1978 Valley. Where are you, seven ball? What paradise have you escaped to? I love Shoe Clue. I love the

Beauty and the back alley, the billions of pieces of broken glass. And I love the Sacred Sink. Oh, how I love this sink. I love this whole bar, the entire crumbling operation. Most of all, though, I love the people. I love Gigi and Mr. John and Penny and her annoying little nephew and Edgar and Pancake and Lana and any other person willing to spend time in here and kill themselves slowly. I love all of you. I really do. My only hope is that you can come to feel this on your own, that you can hear these things being shouted by my heart, because you'll never hear it from me....

There was a brief silence.

Flies buzzed, the popcorn machine hissed.

Pancake leapt down from the bar and slapped me. "Rain!" he shouted.

Lana rubbed my back in support, her eyes half-closed. "That was really nice," she said.

"Good boy, good boy," mumbled Mr. John as he headed back to the front door.

Penny clapped very slowly, perhaps sarcastically. This made the baby cry.

The strangers left the bar.

Edgar hustled back into the kitchen. Something was burning.

Gigi hugged me.

Rum, I told her.

The rum.

Made in the USA
Coppell, TX
16 October 2022

84764628R00111